Chasing Demons

M. E. Layton

Published by Moon Maiden Books

ISBN-13: 978-0692476482
ISBN-10: 0692476482

Chasing Demons

Cover concept and design by Mary Layton/Blue Moon Atelier and Brigid Ashwood

Moon Maiden Books

www.moonmaidenbooks.com

www.facebook.com/MELaytonBooks

For my family - the Becks, the Laytons, and the Clemensons - who have always supported my artistic endeavours.

Chapter One

The demon hunter didn't know I was in love with him when he left me on that cold, rainy December day. Whether those of a particular faith would say the rain was heaven crying at the havoc wreaked by the demon we'd recently vanquished, or hell crying at having to take the demon back was anyone's guess.

If I'm being honest, I don't think I even knew for certain that I was in love with him then. At least, I hadn't admitted as much to myself yet. It had been a wild and hectic few weeks, from the moment the demon hunter walked through the door of my shop until the moment he blinked out of existence. Well, that is, he still existed…somewhere. Just not here, and not now. You see, he's not just a demon hunter. He is a time-traveling demon hunter. And yes, I know how crazy that

1

sounds, trust me. I own a metaphysical, or 'witchy' shop as I like to call it, so I am used to the odd, the weird, the out of this world. I am also a witch. A *real* one. But time travel is not any magic I know of.

It was October when I first met the demon hunter. Samhain to be precise, more mundanely known as Halloween. It is the pagan new year and a time to transition to the coming darkness of the winter months. As it happens, the full moon fell on the 31st of October this year, which made it particularly auspicious for us pagan folk. I was having an open house at the shop - "Celebrate the Samhain Full Moon in the Garden at Morgaine's Grove with officiant Morgaine Clemenson". Morgaine is my magical name. I don't share my real name with very many people because names have power, and a witch needs to protect herself. Magical names have power, too. In fact it is legend in our family that the original Morgaine - or as she's often called, Morgan le Fae - of Avalon and Camelot fame, was the founder, protector, and patron deity of my family's lineage and coven. It is a connection I that consider to be a great honor.

Morgaine's Grove does indeed have a garden - two, actually. My shop with its upstairs flat is situated on a lovely large bit of land just over the road from the beach in a small hamlet between two larger towns along the Outer Banks of North Carolina. There are several similar buildings along this stretch of beach road, but I'm currently the only shop-owner taking advantage of the upstairs area as a residence instead of extra storage or shop space. The public garden, where store-sponsored events and rituals are held, is accessible via a flower-lined walkway to the back of the building. The private garden is smaller, quaint and cozy like an English cottage garden, and is accessible only from my private quarters. The entirety of the gardens is surrounded by a privacy fence, with my private garden walled off from the public portion. Having the fence also protects my plantings from the near constant, sometimes harsh, salty ocean breeze and allows me to grow a few nice plants that would not otherwise thrive in this area.

It was just past 11:30 pm that Samhain night, and most of my friends and clientele had departed for other gatherings, or their own personal rituals. I was closing then, with plans for my own midnight solitary ceremony, looking forward to the quiet ritual of healing and grounding I'd planned. Brighid Pratchett, my closest friend, was the last to leave after having helped me tidy up. I watched and waved as she turned the corner toward her home. I'd always felt her long, wavy ginger hair, tall pre-Raphaelite figure, and exquisite Stevie Nicks dress sense made her look more like a witch shop proprietress than me. My hair, albeit long and wavy, was fine and mousey. I try for the whole gypsy-boho skirts and scarves look, but being on the short side, ankle length skirts usually brush the floor on me and sort of diminish the look.

I slipped back into the shop, easing the door closed to lock up. That's when he appeared. A broad, muscular torso seemed to materialize from nowhere in the ten or so inches of opening between the door and its frame. I glanced up. Beneath a head of shoulder-caressing wavy dark hair was a strong, smiling face featuring glittering blue eyes. Our eyes locked, his blue ones drawing in my green-eyed gaze, and a frisson ran through me. His surprised expression matched my own, and suggested he felt that same shock of connection too. But, he was a stranger, and I fought to put my guard back up and break the stare.

"Sorry!" he said, recovering himself. "If I could just borrow you for a moment?" He was English. I like the English. Love that accent. My parents moved here from England just before I was born - I tend to spout the odd Briticism myself, like calling my home a 'flat', for instance. But, I was a bit wrong-footed by his sudden appearance, and disconcerted by that jolt of connection.

"I'm...I'm just closing," I said, not opening the door further. "We'll be open again in the morning..."

"That might be too late," he interjected. "Won't take a moment. Please?"

Annoyance warred with curiosity as we stood there looking at each other, him smiling so charmingly and beseechingly - I was focusing on his lips, avoiding those piercing eyes. "Really? Can't it wait until tomorrow? It's been a long day, I've got a ritual planned, followed by tea and biscuits, and cuddling with my cat."

His smile didn't falter. "I really must be clear - it is rather an urgent matter. I was told that if you were reluctant, I should appeal to you by your sigil, the Ivory Raven."

That did it. Fewer people knew of that than know my real name. The Ivory Raven is the sigil of my family, and therefore our coven, and has been since our earliest association with the legend of Morgaine's patronage. It was said that when the Isle of Avalon disappeared forever, an ivory raven emerged from the fading mists and flew to my ancestor - a sign that all was well and that Avalon and its inhabitants were safe. I narrowed my eyes at him. "Who are you, and how do you know about that?"

"Please," he cast a glance back out into the street, "perhaps not in the open doorway?" As far as I could tell there was no one else nearby, no other sounds but those of the ocean over the road tickled my ears.

I hesitated only momentarily before stepping aside and allowing him to enter. If he knew my sigil, chances were that he was no threat to my well-being, so I closed and locked the door behind us, pulled the shade, and motioned for him to follow me to the private office I kept in the back. I was at least going to have my cup of tea.

The soft glow from the dimmed lights of the storeroom lead the way to the office. My office sits in the corner that looks out over the public garden, partially beneath the stairs that lead up to my flat. The door was open and the light filtering through the windows from the moon was almost enough to navigate the room by, but I turned on the overhead light and motioned my visitor toward my little sitting area in the back corner by the window looking out over the garden. It was in a cozy little nook created by the rise of the stairs and the landing where they turned back toward the shop area as they lead up to the flat. My guest made his way over, turning his gaze from me to the direction of travel just in time to barely miss banging his head on the sloped wall. Amused, I quickly looked away as he deftly ducked to his left and chose the chair farthest from the slope. I turned my attention to tea making, picking up my electric kettle with the intention of filling it from the tap in the storeroom. It was already full. Odd...I didn't recall having filled it, but with all the bustle of preparations for the party, I was not overly surprised. I popped it back on the warmer, turned it on and set about prepping the tea cups.

"You'll have some tea, won't you?" I grabbed the milk from my mini-fridge.

"Yes, please. I'd love a cup."

"Right, then. You've got some explaining to do..." I prompted.

"Where to start? Um...my name is Alexander Ramsey and I need your help...as a witch."

"Please don't tell me you've interrupted my relaxing evening plans because you need a love potion!" The kettle finished boiling and I poured the water over the teabags to steep. "There really isn't any such thing, you know."

"No, no! Nothing like that, I promise you! No, this is something rather more serious." I heard him shifting in his chair. "Now, before I go on, I want to ask you to please keep an open mind, because I know this will sound beyond the realm of possibility."

I stopped fussing with the tea and turned to face him.

He fidgeted again. "I'm not from here."

I couldn't help myself laughing. "Yeah, I got that from the accent."

He shook his head, chagrined. "What I mean is I'm not from here, or from now."

I lifted an eyebrow. Well, I tried to. What I actually did was lift both of them, because I've never been able to master lifting only one at a time. However, I digress.

"I am from England. But, I'm from England in the year 1892."

I stared.

"Um. I'm a time traveler."

"OK," I started toward the door. "I'm not sure how you heard about me or my sigil, but I think maybe you need to leave." If this was Brighid's idea of trying to set me up with a lonesome loser, no matter how handsome he might be, I was going to hex her into next week.

He stood, but didn't move from the sitting nook. "I told you it would sound impossible, but I assure you, I am not mad. I am telling the truth, and time travel is possible, but of course there are rules, and restrictions to keep the timeline intact."

I stepped over to my desk and reached for the phone.

"No, please - wait! I'll prove it to you! Look -" he closed his eyes for a second and his entire body…blinked. As if he were a light that someone had turned off and right back on again. "There," he said. "I just popped back about 20 minutes ago to fill the kettle for you."

"Oh, *please!*" Weird blinking illusion or not, I wasn't falling for...but then a memory flashed into my mind. I was standing in the shop with the last of my guests and there he'd been - crossing behind Brighid and a couple of customers sipping punch, nodding to me and walking out the door. Within this new memory, I'd just assumed he'd drifted in and out like any other customer. But, it was definitely him, and given the direction he'd been walking when I noticed him, he could very well have come from the storeroom after having topped up my kettle. And I am certain I had not seen him during the party until just now.

I felt dizzy. As I gave my head a shake, he appeared at my side, taking my elbow and gently leading me over to the sitting nook, his other hand lightly around my waist. "Sorry about that. It can be disconcerting to have a memory flip."

"Memory flip? I don't...um...Mr...Mr..."

"Alex. Please call me Alex." He settled me into one of the chairs and crossed over to the tea table. "How do you take it?"

"How am I supposed to take it?" I mumbled.

"Oh! No, I meant the tea. How do you take your tea?"

"I, um," I huffed out a silly giggle. "Just milk, please." I leaned forward and put my head in my hands while the dizziness passed. When I looked up, he was placing teacups on the little table between the chairs. He'd even plated up a few of the dark chocolate Hob Nobs I'd ordered from a British foods importer. I felt movement around my ankles and looked down to see that Pippin Severus Sagan, my cat, had decided to investigate the commotion downstairs. "Oh, hey Pip." I reached down to scratch him behind the ears. He wound his way around my ankles and settled in front of my feet to study the intruder sitting in what he considered to be *his* chair.

"Ah, Pip is it?" Alex leaned forward and slowly extended his hand. "Sorry for the disruption." He glanced up at me. "Cats, as you probably know, have a keen sensitivity to magic, but also to disturbances in other planes that people generally are unaware of."

I nodded, still a bit disoriented. I watched Pip - he was an excellent judge of character, and if he trusted Alex, then I knew I could as well. Pip gave Alex's fingers a quick sniff and then head-butted his hand. Well, he was all right by Pip, then. I reached for my tea and took a soothing sip. "OK. Let's say I believe you, and let's face it, that was pretty convincing. How do you do that? Is it some kind of magic? I've never heard of a spell that -"

"Oh, it's not a spell. At least, not in any way you would be familiar with. It's...I can't explain it, really. We don't know if it is derived from some extra-terrestrial technology, or some sort of ancient magic we can't know of in the present time."

"Alien technology? Highfalutin talk for someone from 1892."

"Well, I am a time-traveler, so I suppose you could say," he grinned, "I've been exposed."

"How far into the future have you been?!"

He considered for a moment. "I shouldn't really divulge too much, but...well, some few years hence." He quickly added, "But, don't even think of asking me to tell your future - I couldn't even if I wanted to."

"Mmhmm. How did you come to be in possession of a method of time travel in 1892?"

"That is an interesting tale. The short version is that I was contacted by another time traveler, who became a mentor of sorts. Someone from a much earlier time and a founder of the society which I am a member of. There is a connection to your patron, actually."

"Morgaine? She...she really existed?" I was gobsmacked, as my mother likes to say. My family's coven goes back centuries, and even though our patron was said to be Morgaine, we were never completely convinced that it was actually THAT Morgaine. I mean, of course there's a possibility that Arthur was a real person, or at least that the exploits of several warrior kings or princes became the legend. "She is part of our coven's origin story, but we always thought Morgaine of the Fae was part of the fantasy, and that our Morgaine was just a contemporary of those times, given that name in the tales handed down through our generations for the Avalonian association."

"Oh, she was...is, quite real, although many of the legends are certainly misguided at best, some even invented for storytelling value or political expediency. But Morgaine, Avalon - very real."

"Wow." I watched as Pip hopped up into Alex's lap and settled in as if his thighs had been made for a cat ornament. Regardless of Pip's obvious approval, I remained a little wary that this guy might just be a good con artist. I am well enough versed in magic and the paranormal not to dismiss him out of hand, however. I had so many questions, but his next statement derailed my queries.

"She is the one who instructed me to mention the Ivory Raven to you, actually."

I nearly did a spit-take with my tea. "She…knows who I am?!"

"Well, she is a very powerful witch. And, of course, a time traveler - one of the first."

Morgan le Fae - Morgaine, the Lady of Avalon, half-sister to King Arthur - or whatever the truth of it actually is, knows who I am. Had she traveled to this time period? Had I actually met her and not known it? Was she one of the coven members, several of whom were of my mother's generation and who I only saw on the major sabbats? Would Alex tell me if I asked? I could probably guess the answer to that question.

"Me being a time traveler is only part of it, though. There is something else you need to know - the reason I need your skills and your magic."

Uh-oh. There was that dark cloud of ominous foreboding. "You might as well lay it all on me, skippy."

His brow furrowed. "Skippy? Maybe that mind flip was more disorienting than I thought." He leaned forward slightly and said slowly and clearly, "My name is Alex. Alex Ramsey."

This time I laughed with abandon, which seemed to worry him even more. I looked down to see Pip giving me side-eye from his perch on Alex's lap. "No, no - I know. Skippy is…kind of a nickname, it can be a term of endearment among friends."

"Ah, I see!" He looked immensely relieved, and amused, but then he turned serious again. "Now, to the crux of it. This time traveling, it isn't just for a lark, you understand. It is quite serious business."

I sat up straighter and gave every indication of listening intently.

"There are forces in the world, forces from other planes of existence which can sometimes impact this world. You know of lesser demons, of course. Imps, bogarts, flibbets, alps, pucks…those sorts of things. Minor demons that are easily dispatched with a ward, or a few words of banishment. They tend to pester people when they get bored, and just as easily tire of that activity and return to their own planes."

I nodded. "I've encountered some, yes." Not that I'd actually seen their physical forms, but I had definitely experienced their pranks and antics and had banished my share of them.

"In ancient times, people with great magical power within our world banished demons to a different plane of existence, one that exists in concert with our own, the human plane. There are varying levels of hierarchy on this demonic plane, and heavily warded gates to prevent higher demons, or major demons as we usually call them, from crossing back into the human plane. At best, the major demons can merely send a lesser demon to persecute a human they may have taken a disliking to, or a group of humans just for the spite of it. Lesser demons are not restricted to just the demonic plane however, as much as we might like them to be. They've never interfered successfully in the evolution of the planet and were thought to be not worth worrying about. As for the major demons since that time, the only access previously to our plane on their own has been if they have been summoned by name and invited to possess the body of a willing human, and then, their powers are severely confined, and their strength limited to that of their human host. They can, of course cause quite a bit of damage using the adrenal functions to boost the strength of their human host, but they can do no real harm to the grand order of the human world."

Something occurred to me then, and I needed to know. "What happened in September 2001. Do you…are you aware of the attacks?" He nodded. "Was that demons possessing those men who hijacked the planes? Because, that was pretty harmful to the grand order of the human world."

"No." He shook his head. "I am afraid those men were all too human."

Of course. I knew that, but I still wished for something other than pure, misguided human hate on which to lay blame.

"Couldn't you, or another time traveler have stopped it?"

He glanced down. "There are some things we can not do. There are certain restrictions that prevent us - physically prevent us - interfering in certain events, no matter how much we might wish to."

I sighed, exasperated. "Let me guess, it's like on Doctor Who, right? Fixed point in time?" Being a child of English parents, I grew up with the Doctor. Alex looked confused. "Never mind. Sorry. I had to ask."

"It's okay." He took a sip of his tea, "but, yes, I suppose 'fixed point in time' is as accurate a description as any."

"What about what just happened - when you went back to fill the kettle and I had the…the memory flip? Was that not against the rules?"

"I needed to prove to you that I am really a time traveler," he shrugged. "That little bend of the rules is allowed under certain circumstances."

"OK…" I supposed that made sense. "Now, about these major demons, you said their 'only access previously'…"

"Yes. Very observant. Something has happened to the wards on one of the gates. There is…a leak, so to speak. It is allowing major demons to gain access to the human plane without having been summoned and without need of a willing human body to possess."

"That can't be good."

"It very much isn't." He set his teacup down and stroked Pip for a thoughtful time before continuing. "That is why I am here. I'm not just a time-traveler, I am a time-traveling demon hunter. And I am here because there is a demon loose. The transition to our plane has weakened it, and it must be stopped before it gathers its full strength."

"And you need something from me?" I prompted when he seemed reluctant to continue.

"I do." He nodded slowly. "I need bait."

"You what?"

"I need you to help me trap the demon. It is a complicated issue. We…members of my society…we can vanquish the demon once it is trapped, but we can not trap them ourselves." He flapped a hand in the air. "Rules and restrictions and that. It requires a powerful witch, freely willing to act as bait with the magical skill to then entrap the demon for us once it is drawn to her or him. There is some good news," his lips quirked up at one corner, not entirely reassuring. "Any time a demon transitions to this plane, it is weakened somewhat, but because it is Samhain, and the veil between the planes of the living and the dead is thinner, we have a slight advantage. Those from this area with magical essences who have passed on will have sensed the presence of the demon and attempted to repel it. Unfortunately, even en masse, their status as departed spirits mean that their powers will not have been enough to send it back to its own plane, but fighting the dead will have further weakened the demon."

"How many of these demons have you sent back so far?"

"Two."

"Just two?"

"Well, this is a recent occurrence, this leak. And since the demons can come through at any time or place in our timeline, it has been hard to track them. We have finally managed a warning ward that will alert us when it happens, but until then it was just a matter of picking up on altered timelines to know that we had a demon on the loose. Once the demon is at full strength and active it is very difficult to send them back. My mentor wished to protect me, to carry on the work, therefore I have only been on two missions so far, and those were to vanquish demons we detected before they reached full strength."

I sat back in my chair and fixed him with a look. "Extremely dangerous, is it?"

"Yes."

"Low chance of success?"

"Well, fair to middling."

"Low pay?"

"…No pay, actually."

"Saving the world with no hope of recognition?"

"Not a chance."

I stood and offered him my hand. "Let's do this."

Chapter Two

Maybe I should be ashamed to admit it, but I'm not. I Googled him.

Before falling into an exhausted sleep that night, I propped myself up in bed with my laptop, Pip purring by my side, and did some research. I accepted what Alex had told me, but I was still cautious and, mostly, curious. Time travel. Who'd have thought it would actually be possible? Obviously I didn't expect him to be on the first page of results unless he'd been someone of importance in his time. After digging for a bit, I did find references to someone who might have been him on one of the genealogy sites. Alexander Charles John Ramsey, born in London in 1859, son of Charles, Viscount Ramsey and Anna Jane Cox. He served as a Lieutenant in the Royal Navy and was listed as missing, presumed dead after the boat he was on was lost at sea due to a mishap during naval exercises in 1892. That fit in with the chronology of his becoming a time traveler. The loss of the ship would have provided excellent cover for his disappearance. I only hoped that the accident had been something that was going to happen and couldn't have been interfered with as opposed to something Alex's time traveling mentor caused. Somehow, I felt it must have been the former, as a group of people dedicated to preserving life would not be likely to cause innocents to die just to cover up a recruitment. On further researching, I discovered that Alex was in fact the only crewman lost. It was presumed that he went down with the ship after seeing the rest of the complement to safety - strongly insisting the captain go before him on the last lifeboat, manhandling the man into the boat by one account. An act of insubordination that got him demoted to Sub-Lieutenant and, at the same time, awarded the Conspicuous Gallantry Medal. No mention of a wife or children.

The next morning, I called Brighid and asked her to come watch the store for me for an hour or so. I had agreed to meet Alex for breakfast so he could fill me in on the demon. Also self-employed, a successful web site designer and coder, Brighid often brought her laptop and worked from here anyway when she wanted a change of scenery. She was a bit reluctant this time, until I told her I was meeting a guy I'd met after last night's party for breakfast.

"SO!! Tell me all about him," she breezed through the door, flipping the sign from "open" to "closed" and pulling the shade down in one fluid movement.

"Woman. I just opened," I snapped. The morning's hastily consumed coffee had yet to work its magic.

"I'll re-open, soon as you spill. Is he tall, dark, and handsome? Blond surfer-dude type?" She lowered the tone of her voice and made a serious face, "Very important business man?" and back to standard best-friend insistence, "What? Who?!"

"Shut up, and I'll tell." I closed the till, having insured the correct starting funds were in place for making change. "Right. He's nice."

"You gotta give me more than that!"

"All right, all right!" Still snappish, I was not really in the mood for an interrogation. "His name is Alex. Dark hair, longish. Medium height, blue eyes, fit. He's English."

"OH. MY. GOD!" She's a sucker for a foreigner. "THAT ACCENT!! Amirite?"

I swear sometimes she should have been a teen in the 80s, a "Valley Girl" with blond hair, living on the west coast. But no, my friend had been pre-teen further inland in the 80s.

"Yes, it's a very nice accent." I had to give her some story, or she'd never let me be. I couldn't exactly tell her we'd be making plans to vanquish a demon over breakfast, so I decided to borrow a bit from my searching last night. "He's a former Royal Navy officer. He's here in the States doing some research on the area's maritime past." That should suffice. With the east coast's long naval history, from Blackbeard's

21

exploits to the naval activities of the Revolutionary and Civil wars, it is quite possible a person who'd served in the Royal Navy would be in town and interested in that sort of thing. "I agreed to help out."

She paused from setting up her laptop on the counter and laughed. "Really? And what do you know about maritime history?"

Not much of anything, as well she knew. "Well, I know where the local museums and libraries are."

"MmmHmmm…" she cut her eyes at me. "And that required a breakfast meeting?"

"Yes, Brighid. A breakfast MEETING." She was eager for me to find a partner. I'd not been serious with anyone in nearly a decade. I just wasn't, you know, *looking* for a relationship. There were…encounters. That was enough for now. Besides, there aren't a lot of guys, especially in this part of the US, commonly referred to as the "bible belt" who would be open to having a witch for a girlfriend. Also, it was likely that her opinion of my lack of relationship was colored by her own love life. She LOVED men, loved the attention, loved the idea of being in love. Normally, that would be a recipe for repeated heartbreaks leading to an eventual broken spirit, but Brighid always bounced back. She seemed to be ruled by her hormones, and that's just the way she liked it.

"And, I don't really know a whole lot more about him," I continued - a tiny obfuscation, "because we only met last night. That's why I promised to meet him for breakfast." I glanced at the wall clock. "Which I am now five minutes late for."

"Go, go!" Brighid flapped me toward the door. "Flip the sign on your way out, wouldja?"

I t was only a five minute walk to the pier where we'd agreed to meet. There is a cafe at the base of it, with a large al fresco dining area out front and limited seating inside. Most people ate outside anyway during the season, but in the cold months there was plenty of indoor seating for just us locals. It was still mild enough for eating outside in early November, with the added bonus of fewer flies. Sloped walkways curving up either side of the cafe allowed access to the pier. I saw him seated on the cafe patio just before he noticed me. He wore the same slacks and white button-down shirt as the night before, but today his hair was pulled back into a low ponytail and tied with a red ribbon. A little sizzle of energy zinged through me, a remnant of the spark I'd felt when we'd locked eyes the previous night.

Like a true gentleman (and officer) he stood and pulled a chair out for me. "Good morning. Sleep well?"

"Yeah, mostly…some weird dreams."

"To be expected. A memory flip can throw the brain off slightly just afterward. What would you like for breakfast?"

"Another coffee would be heavenly! Just cream, no sugar," I glanced over at the large menu on the cafe's front. "Mmm, bacon, and eggs scrambled with cheese, please." Remembering that he wasn't from around these parts, I reached for my purse. "Do you need cash?"

"Oh, no - we have ways of making provision for whatever time period we find ourselves in. This is my treat." he gave me a dazzling smile before heading to the cafe to order.

Streaky clouds were giving way to the sun as it hovered above the horizon, warming the air. The light sea breeze was still fresh, though, and I was glad I'd worn my cardigan and a lightweight scarf. Not wanting to be caught staring, I pretended to be focused on the surf and watched from the corner of my eye as Alex returned from putting in our order. He was a striking man. Well-built, but not overly muscular. He carried himself well, standing tall, broad shoulders back and head held high. Brighid would certainly approve, were she here.

"Shouldn't be too long," he said, settling next to me at the round table. "It seems rather quiet, doesn't it?"

"It's off peak. There won't be many tourists left."

"Probably for the best, given current circumstances. We should act as quickly as we can. Our luck with Samhain notwithstanding, the sooner we can track and vanquish the demon, the better for everyone…especially us. They are weaker during the day as well, so we'll want to make a start before nightfall."

"I wouldn't even know where to begin." I fiddled with the fringe on my scarf. "I've never dealt with anything more than simple hauntings, bad ju-ju, Mercury retrograde…that sort of thing."

"I know, and I'm sorry that there may not be a lot of time to get you up to speed. There never is really. For all our gifts when it comes to time travel, we can't predict when this is going to happen with any real accuracy."

"You said there was a leak. Do you know where the leak is and is there any way to fix it?"

He shook his head. "No, unfortunately. There are others working to find out where the leak is, and once we've found it we will certainly do all we can to seal it, but until then our best hope is to catch a demon breaking through and send it back before it gains enough strength to do massive harm."

"Do you know who…or, I dunno - what this demon is?"

"Not specifically. We're hoping to eventually improve our detection methods to allow us more information of that sort from the start. Our first order of business is a tracking spell. Once we've got a bead on it, we should know more." A waiter approached with our breakfasts and we tucked in. Somehow, I figured I'd better eat while I could - who knows if there'd be regular meals until the demon was dealt with.

"So," I said, after a few satisfying bites, "I'm guessing I'm the one doing the tracking spell?"

He nodded. "I'll help however I can. Once we've tracked the demon, though, you'll have to get its attention. Then, I can only wait until it is trapped, at which point I can begin the vanquishing."

"I suppose I need to know how to get its attention, and what to do once I've got it."

He nodded. "Getting its attention won't be too hard. Once we know where it is, you simply need to cross its path and it will sense you. Anything within about two hundred yards of it should be sufficient for it to notice you. It will be best to have your trap ready before you attract its attention, though, if that is possible. If the demon were to catch you unawares, it could strip you of your power and absorb it for its own use. You will want to set some strong protection wards before you attempt to trap it."

"Now you're being interesting. How do I trap the sucker?"

"That's the tricky part. There is no one way. It will depend on the demon, on your strengths as a witch, and on your collection of spells."

I nodded. "Coming from a long line of witches, I've got a healthy library of spells, which should be helpful."

"If there isn't one already known to you that will suffice, I'm sure you will be able to fashion one based on something in your repertoire."

I certainly hoped so. We finished our breakfasts in silence. I was wracking my brain for entrapment spells, but I'd never had to use one before. Plenty of binding spells came to mind, but I didn't think those would be of any help. I would need to consult the family Book of Shadows. Surely down the centuries my forebears would have had need of a trapping spell, or something near enough that I could adapt it. I became aware that Alex was looking at me with a bit of a smirk. "What?"

"You have this funny little wrinkle in your forehead."

"Oh, that! You mean my Klingon ridge. My friend is always pointing it out when I'm thinking or frustrated or stressed."

"Klingon?"

Right - time traveler, born in the mid 1800s, he probably wouldn't know about Star Trek if he hadn't encountered it in his previous travels. I'd have to get used to that. "It's um…never mind, maybe I can show you what I mean when we've got time."

"I look forward to it."

There was one aspect of his time-travel career we'd not yet discussed. "Can you tell me how this time travel thing works?"

He smiled, "I'm not a physicist, so even if I knew them, I couldn't really lay out all the mathematical formulae that make it possible..."

"Well, no, I didn't expect a physics lesson." I swirled my coffee around in my cup. "I just wanted to know what you do to make it happen. I mean, you said it wasn't a spell, so do you have a thingamajig that you flip a switch on or something?"

"Ah..." he reached a hand into his shirt and pulled out an amulet. It was approximately an inch and a half in diameter and affixed around his neck with a leather cord. It looked, at a glance, like a clay casting and featured an elaborately designed triskele, it's arms reminiscent of acanthus leaves, with a triquetra within its center. "This is my Tempus Purus. It is bound to me and facilitates my ability to travel in time."

"It's beautiful. May I?" I reached out a hand tentatively. Alex nodded and I extended a couple of fingers to caress the surface of the design. When my fingers made contact a jolt of energy shot through me. I felt a tingling run up my arm and spread throughout my body, accompanied by the distinct impression of an intelligence probing my mind. I jerked my hand back in shock. It was definitely not clay, but I couldn't say what it was made of other than some sort of stone or marble, perhaps.

Alex grinned. "Sorry, I probably should have warned you. The Tempus Purus is sentient. It's psychically connected to me as well as being physically bound to me."

"It seems a bit risky, just a leather cord around your neck to keep it on. What happens if it falls off, or gets pulled off?"

Alex flicked open a few buttons on his shirt. "Ah, but when I say it is physically bound to me…" He let the amulet fall back against his chest. I watched, stunned, as it seemed to melt into his skin, amulet and leather cord both. Within seconds, it was gone, the only evidence of its existence a raised replica of the triskele design on his chest, as if it had been embossed there.

"That…that is amazing," I said. "So, what do you do when you're not vanquishing major demons? What sort of job is time traveler normally?"

"Observation. Ours began as a scholarly pursuit, seeking to learn more about the human race, chronicling what makes us tick, I guess you could say."

"Have you ever had trouble with one of your society changing history?"

"Oh my goodness, no. That would not be tolerated. That is why there are all sorts of rules and restrictions. As I mentioned last night, physical restrictions, even. We can't do anything to alter history no matter how much we may want to. Morgaine was instrumental in crafting the wards that enforce the restrictions."

"Oh, so you haven't always been in the business of protecting the human race?"

"Well, yes and no. Not in the way that we have been since this demonic breach of planes. We keep records about the various stages of humanity from the earliest known times, and we even maintain an extensive collection of what makes the human race what it is - objects, texts. I guess you could say we've mostly been curators of humanity. Being made up of many with a talent for magic has left us open to divining alterations in the natural order. So, when this breach happened, it was our wise-people who noticed, and it just seemed the proper thing to do - to try and restore order." He pulled a pocket watch - a POCKET WATCH, for goodness sake, from his trousers pocket. "Now, we should make some plans. I suggest we meet at your shop this afternoon. What time do you close?"

"Normally 5 p.m., but I can close earlier if necessary."

"That might be wise. We should try to have a tracking spell in place before nightfall. I can only imagine that any necessary herbs and magical equipment will be readily to hand since you own a shop specializing in such things." His smile was nice. There was a wee dimple in his right cheek, and those crinkles around the eyes suggested he laughed often. His kind eyes lingered on me, his expression contemplative. My heart beat a little faster under his regard, and before we could repeat the piercing locked gaze of the night before, I looked away and started gathering my things, feeling the heat of a blush rising to my cheeks.

"I'll close up early and start prepping my ritual space." I said, a little too quickly. I'd never got round to having my Samhain ritual last night, so I planned to do a meditation before Alex got there, because I obviously needed to ground myself. "What time should we start?"

"How about 4? Will that give you enough time to prepare?"

"Perfect."

group of giggling teenage girls were leaving when I returned to the shop. I wondered why they weren't in school.

"School newspaper staff," Brighid said, answering my unasked question as I entered. She held up a piece of paper. "I told them you'd be in touch if you were interested in placing an ad."

I placed the coffee and pastry I'd brought her from the cafe onto the counter.

"Oh, you are a peach," she said. "Now," she patted the stool beside her, "Plant your butt and tell me EVERYTHING!"

I shook my head and sat down next to her. "It went just fine. He's very nice, a gentleman. He's looking forward to hitting some of the places I recommended."

She blotted her lips with a napkin, careful not to smudge her lipstick. "When are you seeing him again?"

"Um…no plans."

"AH HA!" She squealed. "You ARE seeing him again!"

"Maybe." I allowed. "But, really, you're making a bigger deal out of this than it is." I fought to keep myself from blushing, recalling the way I'd felt when he'd looked at me before we parted. If Brighid suspected I was attracted to him, even just the tiniest bit, I'd never have a moment's peace from her.

"Mora," that was her nickname for me, "live a little for crying out loud. Is he handsome?"

"Well, yeah, but-"

"What's the hesitation? You're a beautiful woman, Mora."

"Just because you're eager to marry me off doesn't mean Alex is interested in being the prize catch."

"Mmmm," she purred. "First-name basis…"

"Oh, Brighid, leave it out!"

She laughed. "Your British is showing." I didn't really have my parents' accent, but I tended to throw out Briticisms even more when I got a bit agitated.

I glared at her. "Why are you so bloody intent on getting me into a relationship? I'm perfectly happy with the status quo. I *like* my solitude."

"Solitude's one thing, loneliness is another."

"I'm not lonely!!"

"Mora, I know you. You aren't meant to be alone in this world. You were made for better things than spinsterism. Is that a word?"

I shook my head at her. "Probably not."

"Anyway, I can't wait to meet him! When's that happening?"

Hell. I hadn't considered I'd have to make introductions. Though I guess that would be the natural course of things if he were going to be around for a while, even if he were just a friendly visitor to the area, and not a time traveling demon hunter who was handsome, and looked at me like — *Dammit, pull yourself together, Clemenson!* I admonished myself. I shrugged at Brighid in what I hoped was a nonchalant manner. "Well, I mean, I don't know if he's going to hang out much, you know."

"Oh, yeah, you like him!" Her ginger waves bounced as she bobbed her head, obviously not convinced by my attempt to act disinterested. "Not to worry. I'll let you set your own pace there. But I will expect regular reports."

I gave in. "Of course." I smiled. She seemed determined to see me in a relationship with this guy. I could keep fighting, but I decided it was easier to let her think what she wanted. If all went to plan, he'd probably be gone in a couple of days anyway, so there was really no sense in me letting myself get any further interested. Brighid really was a good friend, though. It occurred to me then that she could be in as much danger as any of us. She was a witch, too, although not from a family of them like I was. She'd been drawn to the craft as a teenager, and after some silliness with other school friends, she came to accept that witchcraft, while real, wasn't like in the movies. We'd become closer at that time. We'd always had an easy friendship, but I hadn't revealed myself as a witch to her until then. I introduced her to the realities of the craft and she'd studied everything I'd suggested she read and proved an eager student. She and I were the youngest members of my family's coven.

She finished her pastry and tossed the bag in the bin. "You need me to hang around a bit, or are you ready to take over? I told my mom I'd meet her this afternoon for lunch in Edenton. I know it's only about an hour's drive, but I could stand to do some errands first."

"Oh, sure! Off you go!" I hugged her. "Thanks for watching the shop for me, sweetie. Be careful traveling, and hug your mom for me." She closed her laptop, zipped it up in her carrying bag, and saluted me with her coffee cup as she breezed out the door.

I grabbed some paper and a marker and quickly made a sign that we'd be closing early today, then set about tidying shelves - turning labels to face outward, lining things back up neatly, that sort of thing. Busywork. Thursdays were usually slow days anyway, especially when it wasn't tourist season. Here in the south, not a lot of folks went in for this "new agey mumbo-jumbo" sort of thing, so I had only maybe a dozen regular pagan customers. I did have a sizable clientele who came in for candles, potpourri, handmade soaps and lotions, and cooking herbs, though. Even some of the most devout Christians in the area seemed to tolerate me as a misguided but harmless soul who made really nice smelling soaps.

After a quick lunch from my food stash in the downstairs mini-fridge, I spent most of the afternoon between infrequent customers boxing up some mail-order packages. I did pretty well with an online shop selling my hand-made soaps and candles and some other crafty items. Our postal carrier usually came by around 2 pm, so I wanted to be sure all my orders were ready by then as I'd decided to shutter my online shop until this demon business was over with. By 3 pm, I was ready to close and start prepping for Alex's arrival.

My ritual space was a room within the upstairs flat that had a north-facing window. My altar was set up about four feet from the window, and the rest of the floor was clear. The floor was sealed wood, a good natural material for channeling energies, not to mention easy clean-up. I'd commissioned the craftsman who laid the flooring in the room (the rest of the floors in the flat were carpet or linoleum) to use a cooking torch to scorch a 6' circle into the center of the floor, clockwise, while I followed chanting a protection spell. I think he was more bemused than anything but, of course, the extra $100 I paid him probably made it worth his while scooting around on his knees making as smooth a line as he could. I glanced at the circle as I entered the room. He'd done a pretty nice job, actually.

On shelves along the west and south facing walls, I stored ritual items, including salt for casting a circle - I liked the extra physical presence of a barrier when performing rituals, and I also used it for casting a smaller circle around my altar for meditations and less elaborate rituals. I grabbed the salt as I passed. My ritual athame was mounted on a plaque on the east wall, alongside a rack for hanging herbs to dry. In a closet by the door, I kept a shop vac for large rituals and a hand-held vacuum for small ones to suck up the salt, which I then recycled for the next use. My Book of Shadows was located on a built-in shelf just beneath my altar table, wrapped in vintage silk and kept inside a consecrated wooden box with our coven's Ivory Raven sigil embossed into the top. The book had been my mother's and her mother's before her and so on, going back centuries. Every 50 years or so, it had to be re-bound to include necessary additional pages, but always with the original cover, well-preserved using both mundane methods and magical ones.

I poured out a handful of salt and sprinkled it around the altar in as neat a circle as I could manage, did a brief invocation of ancestors and spirit guides to watch over me and guide my meditation, and knelt in front of the altar. Arranging my meditation candles around the Book of Shadows, I took a deep breath, did my best to clear my thoughts, and opened my mind to receive any guidance the spirits deemed fit to send me. Fifteen minutes later, I was none the wiser about my mission, but I was calm and felt ready to begin the quest for a suitable trapping spell. I carried the Book of Shadows over to my reading chair in the corner of the room and set about searching for any spells that might help. There is no index in a Book of Shadows, as spells are generally entered as and when they have been utilized, so there was nothing for it but to skim through the book. I'd read through it enough to know a few places to start, at least. I doubted I'd find anything before Alex arrived, but the sooner I began, the better.

As suspected, there were no definitive trapping spells. Entrapment is generally never a goal in witchcraft and you would mostly want to banish a demon or wayward spirit as opposed to keeping it around, but the further back in time I searched, the closer I got to finding some spells that may be adaptable. In earlier generations, there seemed to be more dealings with darker forces, but whether those forces were actually stronger then, or people's fear was just easier to use as a manipulation tool is debatable. In any event, there were some pretty strong binding spells and repelling spells entered into the book in those times. I bookmarked a couple of the repelling spells as likely candidates for adaptation into strong protection wards for when we began our task in earnest. Not only would we need to protect ourselves from the big nasty we were dealing with, but we would also be susceptible to interference from any lesser demons on the plane that were looking for opportunities to make mischief.

Having had no real success in finding an appropriate trapping spell - although I still had many hundreds of pages to sort through - it was time to head back downstairs to meet Alex. Pip obviously sensed something was up as he hopped down from his favorite napping spot on the sofa and followed me down to the shop. He jumped up onto the ledge by the big picture window where my Samhain/Halloween display was still installed - I made a mental note to find time to change that out - and settled in to peer through the glass. It wasn't long before Pip mewled and I peeked out of the shade on the front door to see Alex strolling toward us. He'd changed into jeans and a knit shirt, and I ascertained that he'd obviously just been shopping, because that adhesive size strip stores put on jeans was still attached.

I opened the door before he had a chance to knock and closed and locked it behind us. Pip appeared from his perch in the window and greeted Alex like an old friend. I reached down and plucked the tag off Alex's jeans. "Been shopping, I see."

"Oh, yes. Well, I couldn't keep wearing the same things, after all. How did your preparations go?"

"Fine. I'm ready to begin." Part of my pre-meditation preparation had been spent cleansing the ritual space, so we were ready to begin as soon as we had our tools sorted. "I haven't had much luck coming up with a trapping spell yet, but since our first order of business is tracking the thing down, I'm hoping I'll have time to figure something out. I don't suppose you can give me any hints about what the other witches did?"

"Not really. They both had to invent their own spells as far as I could tell, based on their experiences and knowledge. As was the case with them, it is best that I don't know much about how you trap the demon. The less I know about that, the better, in fact."

"I don't understand, wouldn't you need to know?"

"No. It really is best if I don't know. Witches can shield their thoughts from demons, you see. As I am not allowed those sorts of powers, any knowledge I have about the trap could be discovered and used by the demon."

"Fascinating."

He nodded. "It is the way things were set up when this problem arose. We have always been a group of non-witches as well as natural witches and trained witches, but when the leak was discovered, there was a moratorium placed on further magical training. I'd never really pursued the magical training, but that was mainly because I was engrossed in the research of humanity and always thought I'd eventually get around to it. But, when I got recruited to hunt the demons, that course of study was cut off from me."

"Never know what you're missing 'til it's gone, huh?" I gave him a sympathetic smile. "Come on out back, you can help me collect the herbs for the tracking spell. We'll use fresh herbs instead of dried ones. I need to collect or use as much as I can from the garden anyway before winter arrives."

"Of course." He followed me through the storeroom and out the door to my private garden. After some deliberation, we settled on angelica, rue, and dill - for inspiration, clear vision, and some protection. I chose some thyme and aloe as well. Before we began the tracking spell, I planned to do a simple protection ward for us. I'd do some heavier protection work once we got to the business of preparing to actually trap the demon and had some idea of what we'd be dealing with. I also planned to make an amulet to give to Brighid, ostensibly as a thank you gift for watching the store for me, but I mainly wanted to protect her as much as I could from whatever may be coming.

I led the way up to my flat from the spiral stairs in the garden. Pip had gone back up the indoor stairs and was waiting for us in the sitting room. This was the largest space in the house, an open plan layout encompassing the kitchen and dining area as well. A hallway led to my bedroom and en suite bath, and to the ritual space. Pip followed us down the hallway. He usually attended my rituals, taking his place in the chair to watch the proceedings. I always felt his cat energy added an additional layer of protection, and had observed him stalking the space from time to time as if making any uninvited spirits aware of their boundaries. As I'd mentioned previously, although I could often sense their presence, I never actually physically saw any supernatural beings. I had no way of knowing it as I set about collecting the tools we would need for our workings, but all that was about to change.

Chapter Three

Dusk was fast approaching as we finished our preparations. Normally I liked to do spell work while sky-clad (or, "nekkid", if you like) but out of respect for Alex's possible Victorian sensibilities, not to mention a bit of shyness on my part, I opted for a lightweight cotton robe. For his part, Alex stripped down to his boxers. "I know a bit about magic and ritual traditions, despite not being a student of the craft," he'd said.

We moved my simple wooden ritual table to the center of the circle and I unfolded one of the tourist maps that are found in abundance around town onto its surface. The map was typical of those found in popular vacation spots, featuring a map of the larger Outer Banks area on one side with a concentrated map of our village on the other, dotted with points of interest, places to eat, and souvenir spots. The advertisements for local businesses that surrounded the borders of the map were extra noise that could conceivably weaken the spell, but I was confident that we could make it work. One of the ads was for my own shop, so I like to think that gave it a bit of a signal boost for us. Trimming the edges off was not an option as there would still be a few ads within the map's artwork, and it would have meant losing parts of the map on the reverse side. In the event we needed to search outside of the immediate village environs, we'd need that larger map area intact.

Pip groomed himself on the reading chair in the corner as I did my preparatory protection invocation. Alex and I stood on either side of my altar with protection candles lit, including one for the protection of familiars - I never leave Pip out of protection spells. Once I felt the spell taking hold, we clapped out the protection candles and I lit some for focus. We were ready for the tracking spell.

"The essence of this spell is to charm the map and pendulum to detect the presence of the demon," I explained. "Ideally, we would be able to find the general area where the demon was hiding, and as we travel closer, our detection should become more accurate, our path narrowed." The only problem was, this sort of tracking spell worked best when you had something that belonged to the entity you were planning to track - a hair or a fingernail, even a piece of clothing would do in a pinch. We had nothing like that. "Since we don't even know what kind of demon, whether male or female, or what sort of powers it possesses, we'll have to start with a general search for non-human presences. That means identifying and dismissing the presence of pets and wild animals and honing in on entities not of this plane of existence."

We would likely pick up the presence of any lesser demons popping in and out of this plane as well. We weren't going to find this thing in one session, of course. But, we had to start somewhere.

"Right," I said. "Now is the time for eating, drinking, using the bathroom, sex—" *The hell did I just say?!* "I mean - anything that might distract you needs to, um…" I could tell he was laughing at me - not out loud, but I could see the amusement in his eyes, "needs to be taken care of." I scraped together as much dignity as I could and stood up straight, with my head high.

There was that lovely smile. "I'm fine, thank you. We can start whenever you like."

I couldn't decide if he not acknowledging what I'd said made it better or worse. "How is it you aren't very Victorian, for being a Victorian gentleman?"

"I prefer to think of myself as just a gentleman," he said. "As would my mother, no doubt. Did you expect me to be prudish, or overbearingly 'male'?" His smile broadened.

"Honestly, I don't know what I expected. But, you do seem more modern in your sensibilities than one might expect of a man born in the era where men were men and women were property, unless they were the Queen."

"Ah," he said. "You see, that's just the thing. My family has the utmost respect for Her Majesty, and women in general. Let me give you a bit of background. My father, Viscount Ramsey, was raised by his mother, grandmother, and two

43

aunts. His father died when he was just 6 years old. Even though the family was well-to-do, his parents had always been very much involved with raising him, not leaving it to governesses and nannies. So, when his father died, all of the women in the family rallied to raise him. He learnt to respect women from a very early age and when he married my mother and they had me, he was very much present in my upbringing. He treated mother as his equal in all things, asking her advice for his business dealings, even. They taught me those same values. So, I have never been the typical 'Victorian gentleman' in that sense. And, of course, traveling as I do, I endeavor to respect the social values wherever, and whenever, I am."

Yep, that made it worse. Never mind, there was work to be done, I could be embarrassed later. Taking up my salt dispenser, which was an old-fashioned diner-style sugar shaker, I traced a line on top of the circle scorched into the floor. After closing the circle, I quickly called the guardians of the four quarters. Once all the formalities were completed we concentrated on the map and pendulum. Intoning the words to the incantation, I watched as many spots on the map began to glow, the tip of the pendulum swinging wildly between them.

"I recognize some of these spots already." I was able to alter the spell as I went to eliminate some spots that I knew were pets, or the wildlife refuges. "This one, for instance," I pointed at the spot over my store, "that's Pip." As I continued, several spots stopped glowing, but there were still too many for the map to be of any real use yet. "OK," I said after several passes, "at this point, I can't eliminate any more areas. We'll have to note which areas still glow and research on foot."

"It wouldn't be safe for you to go. We can't risk that the demon might sense your presence. That could prove disastrous for us."

I nodded. "I can fashion a talisman for you to carry. Given that it would be part of the whole business of finding and banishing the demon, would I be able to teach you a simple incantation to eliminate false positives?"

"I think so. The worst that can happen is that it won't take. In that event, I'll just use this magical implement," he held up a pen and grinned.

I smiled back. "The talisman will be easy enough to make, I can use fur from Pip and I can easily get dog hair and a bird's feather, maybe some fur from a squirrel. That should be enough to fine tune the spell, if it will work for you, to dismiss the presence of creatures from our plane from the map. That will only leave any lesser demons to trigger the tracking spell, and their movements in and out of the plane might actually make most of them easy to spot and dismiss."

As I was considering all of this, I noticed that the spot over my shop started glowing again. "That's odd. I thought I'd eliminated Pip's presence on the map."

"Maybe those advertisements on the map are interfering after all."

I shook my head. "I didn't think they would." I spoke the words dismissing Pip again. The glow flickered, but didn't fade.

I looked up at Alex. He was concentrating on the map. I noticed a movement over his shoulder. Something was floating outside the window. Pip stood beneath the window, facing whatever hovered there, his hackles raised. My sharp intake of breath and a low growl from Pip got Alex's attention and he turned to face the window as well. What hovered there was mostly flesh-colored, close to my own fair skin tone but with a greenish tint. A smattering of fine grey hair topped its head in soft waves. Its ears were pointed, and the bright green eyes were much larger than human eyes, though the head and face were definitely humanoid. At a guess I supposed it to be no more than 5' tall, its body lean with elongated limbs. As we watched, it raised a hand and wiggled its fingers at us. That seemed to bring us out of our shocked stupor, and I began intoning a banishing spell. The entity did not even flinch, which I would have expected it to do in reaction to the force of the spell. It began shaking its head and waving its arms at us, speaking urgently in a tongue I'd never heard before, as if it were trying to tell us something important. Pip hissed and jumped at the window. The creature turned its attention to Pip and my heart skipped a beat. Would my protection ward shield him from whatever this was? My banishing spell faltered. The entity focused on Pip and began speaking to him, first in that strange tongue, but then it sounded as if he were mewling at Pip. I watched as Pip tipped his head to the side, listening. Then, he sat down calmly beneath the window and meowed back at the entity. I looked at Alex. He shook his head and shrugged. This was new to him, as well. After exchanging a few more meows with the creature at the window, Pip looked back at us and mewled.

I took a step toward Pip, but Alex grabbed my arm, keeping me within the circle. "Who…what are you?" he asked, loudly enough to be heard through the glass.

The entity started speaking again, its voice carrying easily to us as if the window were not a barrier, the first few words in that foreign tongue, but eventually in English, "…mean you no harm. I wish to assist."

Alex stepped forward then, just to the edge of the circle. "Since when do lesser demons wish to help the inhabitants of this plane?"

The entity shook its head. "Not demon. *Daemon*." It - or, he, I suppose - started saying something in his own language, but caught himself. "…apologies. Not used to your words. I am called Lingus. I give you my true name as a sign of trust. I am a nature Daemon."

I looked at Alex. "Demon, Daemon…is there a difference?" Most modern references seemed to use the words interchangeably.

"In ancient Greece, a Daemon was a benevolent spirit of nature, but the word is also considered an archaic spelling of demon."

I turned away from the window and leaned closer to Alex. "Do we trust it? It seems to have gained Pip's good will and while I do trust my cat…I don't know. I'm used to demon and Daemon being kind of the same thing."

Alex nodded. "Yes, I know. If it has given us its true name, however, that is indicative of its good will."

"How do we know if that is its true name, though?"

Alex whispered in my ear and at his direction, I raised my hand toward the window "Ausculto, Lingus - invorto!" The entity flipped upside-down and hovered there. I gave Alex a questioning look, my Latin was rusty since I did most of my spell work in English. "You just told him to invert himself," he shrugged. "I do know of that spell, but I can't use it myself."

Lingus bobbed upside down in the window. He didn't seem too perturbed by the - pun possibly intended - *turn* of events.

"He could have faked that, surely," I said.

Alex nodded. "Possibly, but that, and Pip's acceptance makes me think he just may be dealing fairly with us."

A further whisper from Alex and I lowered my hand. "Exsolvo."

Lingus flipped upright again, smiling indulgently as if he fully expected some kind of test. "I give you my word, on my true name: I will not harm you, and wish only to help restore the natural balance of energies." He seemed to be starting to get the hang of English, no longer slipping into his native tongue.

"Well, then. I suppose it can't hurt to talk to him." I quickly dismissed the guardians we'd called, inwardly asking their forgiveness for the abruptness, and opened the circle. Alex and I walked to the window and looked out at Lingus. Pip wound his way around our ankles, as if enclosing us in his own protective circle. "I will let you enter, but you must go no further than this room without my express permission." Lingus bowed his head in acceptance of my terms, and I unlocked and raised the window. He floated gracefully in and gently landed on the floor near my altar. There was just the tiniest fluttering of glowing particles behind him as if he were folding nearly invisible wings into his body. He knelt and held his hand out to Pip, who sauntered over and accepted the attention.

He cooed something in his own language to Pip, a lilting, not unpleasant sound, and looked up at me. "Your companion is very wise and cares for you very much." Pip made his own gentle mewling sounds then. "He wishes you to know that he really prefers that food with the…gravy?"

I nodded. "Figures. The most expensive stuff." It did not escape my notice, the absurdity of discussing my cat's diet with an entity quite possibly from another plane of existence.

Alex leaned against the window sill and studied the visitor. "If you aren't truly a benevolent entity, you are a very determined demon. Any other lesser demon would have tired of the pretense by now."

Lingus stood and folded his hands in front of him. He was dressed in what looked to be rough hewn linen - a belted tunic and simple fitted trousers. No shoes as we know them, but strips of the same material as his shirt, belt, and pants were wound around his feet and ankles. His smile was pleasant, although the animal-like sharpness of his incisors lent an edge to what seemed an otherwise kind expression. "I understand your hesitations. My apologies for my unexpected appearance. It is hard to know what is the best way to make an entrance." His smile widened and he slowly blinked his eyes. He had lashes most women would kill for. "Your spell workings attracted my attention, and I wished to observe. I realized that you must be attempting to find the demon that has made its way to this plane, and I wished to offer my assistance."

Alex nodded. "I don't suppose you know where it is?"

"I am afraid I do not. I have sensed its existence on this plane, but have yet to determine its hiding place. It is, thankfully, very weak still." He tilted his head and studied Alex. "You are…misplaced, as well. Out of this time, I think?"

Alex looked levelly at Lingus. I could tell he still wasn't sure about trusting this creature. "Something like that."

Lingus nodded. "I won't ask for knowledge that you do not wish to give. I ask only that you be open to my good will and extend me a measure of trust." He looked from Alex to me and back again. Pip, sitting now at Lingus' feet, mrr'd as if encouraging our agreement.

Despite the shock of Lingus' sudden appearance, my instincts seemed to be aligned with Pip's. A lifetime of studying the tricksters of fairy lore and mythology, however, made me cautious just the same. But at this point, we didn't have much choice but to accept Lingus' help. He would likely have a better demon radar than either of us, and anything that could make our task easier and faster would be a blessing.

Alex seemed to have come to a similar conclusion. He extended a hand to Lingus. "We would be most grateful for your assistance, Lingus. And, we'll..." he looked at me, "we will work on trusting." I nodded.

Lingus accepted Alex's hand. "I can ask no more of you. My thanks."

"I suppose if we're to be working together, it wouldn't be fair of me to restrict your movements." I gestured toward the doorway. "You are welcome in my home."

Lingus bowed slightly. "Thank you, madam, but as I am a creature of nature, I am most comfortable when not confined by walls and ceilings. If I might have the freedom of your garden to abide when I require shelter, that should be sufficient to my needs."

"Of course."

We spent most of the rest of the night working with Lingus to perfect our tracking spell. He was very helpful in eliminating pets and wildlife from our plane, as he could zip out and back in after checking the "hot spots" within minutes. It would have taken

Alex, even working with my talisman, hours to have accomplished as much. Lingus located several lesser demons for us as well and used his own magic to place harmless tracers on them so that they would manifest in an identifiable way on my map.

"I am unable to sense the location of the major demon," he said. "It is possible that it may have found a blind spot in which to hide. It could be underwater or deep underground, for instance."

"That gives us some information to work with anyway," I said. "At least we know that it can find blind spots on this plane. Thank you, Lingus."

Lingus did not seem to tire, but Alex and I found ourselves struggling to stay awake and concentrate. Any magical workings can take a toll on you. We decided to stop for the night, and I invited Alex to crash on the sofa-bed since it was really late for a taxi, and there was no way he'd have been able to make it back to his hotel on foot without passing out from exhaustion. As tired as I was, I lay in bed for a long while, Pip curled against my back, purring away. So much was happening and not a lot of it made much sense. I was open to all the possibilities of what was happening, of course, but the reality of it was almost overwhelming in these quiet moments. Not only was there a major demon needing vanquishing on this plane, but I had now met - actually met - another creature I'd no idea existed until now. Eventually, sleep came. It was a dreamless sleep, though, and I woke up feeling more rested than I had expected to.

Alex was still asleep, softly snoring, when I tiptoed into the kitchen to make coffee. As it brewed, I made my way down to the shop and replaced the early closing sign from yesterday with one announcing that the shop would be closed for the rest of the week and weekend.

When I came back upstairs, Alex was stirring. "Mmmmmm...that smells lovely." Pip jumped up on his chest, eliciting an "oof!" from him, and started kneading and purring.

"Did you sleep OK?" I pulled some mugs down from the cupboard.

"Not bad, considering. Yourself?"

"Yeah, actually," I'd stuck my head in the fridge to assess breakfast possibilities. "Coffee's on as you've noticed. I've got bacon and eggs if you're interested."

"Fantastic!" he said. I nearly banged my head on a shelf - he'd sidled up behind me. "Sorry! I should have made a bit more noise."

I gave him a stern look. "I don't know how many more surprises I can handle, mister!"

He put his hand over his heart and bowed at the waist. "My sincerest apologies, milady."

A tap at the window caused both of us to start. Lingus hovered outside the kitchen window. I lifted the sash. "G'morning, Lingus."

"Sorry to have startled you, madam. I thought I sensed you stirring and wanted to ascertain that you were well."

"Yeah, we're fine. And, please - call me Morgaine. You want some breakfast?"

"Thank you, no. I have made provisions for my sustenance already." I wasn't sure I wanted to know exactly what that meant. "When you are ready to continue our work, you need only say my name." He floated back down to the garden and disappeared.

I closed the window and turned to face Alex. "I hope he can't hear everything we discuss."

He smiled. "Probably not. He gave us his true name, so he probably only hears us when we speak it."

I turned back to the fridge and got the bacon, eggs, and butter out. "Can you grab a pan from that cupboard there," I said, pointing. When he handed it to me, I put it on the stove and pulled a baking sheet from the drawer beneath the oven. Turning the oven on to heat, I arranged several strips of bacon on the baking sheet and set about preparing the eggs. "I guess we'd better eat while we can. Things are likely to get weird from here on out, I imagine."

"Yes, I suspect so." He busied himself looking in drawers and cupboards, gathering plates and utensils. "I just hope we can catch this beastie at less than optimal strength."

After breakfast was prepared, we sat, serving ourselves from the dishes I'd placed on the table.

"I have a confession to make," I said.

"Mmm?" Alex said, shoveling eggs into his mouth.

"I Googled you." Mistaking his raised eyebrows for confusion, I attempted to explain, "Oh, um, 'Google' is a search engine…" as if he'd know what that meant, "…which is…"

"Oh, I know what a search engine is," he said, saving me from further embarrassment. "I am familiar with contemporary computing devices." He smiled.

"Well, in that case, you probably know what I mean when I say 'I Googled you'."

"I'm not sure I've actually heard that term, exactly, but I surmise it means you researched me?"

I nodded. "Yes. I was curious to see if there was any record of your existence. Sorry, I was still a bit weirded out after your initial appearance."

"I completely understand. I probably would have done the same in your situation."

I sipped my coffee and stirred some salt and pepper into my eggs. "There wasn't a lot of information, but I learned that you were in the Royal Navy when you, um, disappeared."

"Ah. Yes. My infamous 'valorous demotion', as my mentor called it," he laughed. "I've actually seen a letter from my commander to my parents - a personal letter, sent along with the official notice that I was missing and presumed dead. It's in the archives at the…my place of work." I'd noticed he had done that before, not given name to his time travel group. "He was very grateful - off the record, of course - that I'd made him get into the lifeboat ahead of me. He had a wife and two children, you see. I miss him. He was a good friend."

"There was a little about your parents, but no mention of siblings, or other family."

"I was an only child," he said. "My parents always hoped for more, but the 1800s were often unkind on women and childbearing, and my mother never conceived again."

"How about you?" I asked. "Did you marry, have children?"

He smiled sadly. "No. There was an engagement. At that time, there were still instances of arranged marriages, and I was promised to a girl a couple of years younger than me - the daughter of my father's closest friend. Her name was Leonora. We played together as children, and honestly, she was more like a sister to me than a potential mate. But I was very fond of her, and she of me. We would have gone through with the marriage, although, I suspect her…affections…were otherwise intended."

"She was in love with another man?"

"No," he said. "Not another man." His eyes met mine pointedly over the edge of his cup as he took a sip of coffee.

"Oh!" I said, when it dawned on me what he'd meant. "What happened? You said you would have gone through with the marriage…"

"She died," he said, simply. "Tuberculosis, or 'consumption' as it was often called then. In her 15th year."

"I'm so sorry," I said.

"Thank you," he acknowledged with a small smile. "It was hard, losing her. As I said, even if we weren't in love, I did love her as a friend, and I miss her. She did have a happy life, I'm glad to say. Her affections were reciprocated, and both the lady she loved and I were able to visit her at the end. And," he said, brightening, "you know almost all that happened after that! I soon joined the Royal Navy, and after a time, transitioned to this vocation."

Once we'd finished breakfast, Alex headed back to his hotel to shower and change, and I set about my own morning routine. Once I'd showered and dressed, I went downstairs and out the side door into the main garden. I was hoping to find Lingus there, and I was not disappointed. He was kneeling by the little fountain, surrounded by happily chirping birds. His grey hair and physical bearing spoke of a creature of great age, but his large eyes, small stature, and smooth skin lent a youthful air to him. As I approached, the gravel of the path crunching beneath my feet, the birds flew away, startled. Lingus looked up at me and smiled. "Hello, Morgaine."

"I'm sorry I scared your...friends."

"Not to worry. It is best they maintain a healthy fear of humans. Your kindness with providing seed and fresh water has not gone unnoticed, however." His English was much better. Obviously he knew the language. I guess he just didn't have an opportunity to speak it much.

I sat down by the fountain with him. "I hope you understand our hesitance last night. I suppose we are a bit paranoid, what with the demon roaming about."

He smiled. "It is to be expected. And, like the birds, it is best if humans maintain a healthy fear of the supernatural."

I smiled. "You said last night that you are a Daemon. A nature spirit?"

"Yes. We are an ancient race, attuned to all of nature - animals, plant life, sea life. I am a guardian of forests and gardens, but there are others who guard oceans, deserts, tundras, all manner of natural places and things, but we all have an affinity with the whole of the natural world."

"How did you know to come to us? I didn't even know about the demon until a couple of nights ago. Did someone call you forth?" I hoped he wouldn't think me impertinent.

"We - nature spirits - are always observant, always waiting. We can not be called forth by any other being. We can be appealed to, but in times of trouble we either attend, or we do not. But we are always aware."

"But, you've…attended now."

"Yes. When there is a threat as great as this, we attend."

"That doesn't fill me with hope," I said. "It makes me think this could be something we might not be able to handle."

He reached out and placed a hand on my arm. His skin was warm and soft. "You must not despair, Morgaine. I have come to do all in my power to help humans repel this threat."

I noticed a few of the birds had returned and sat on the edge of the fountain observing us. Lingus took note that I'd seen them.

"If you remain still, they will stay nearby. They sense you mean them no harm."

"I've always loved animals. Birdsong in springtime always makes me happy. I make sure to keep Pip - my cat - happy indoors. He loves to watch the birds from the windows, but I think he realizes they are off limits."

We sat in silence for several minutes. The gentle susurration of the fountain soothed me, as did Lingus' peaceful presence. The sense that he was worthy of our trust grew stronger the more time I spent with him. It was clear he was no lesser demon, but I also maintained a healthy respect for him as a creature of nature - likely to be wild and untamed by human standards, no matter how docile he seemed at present.

"I have been in contact with other nature Daemons since last night," he said, breaking the silence. "It is possible that others may join our efforts to rid this plane of the demon."

"Oh. Well, thank you. I can only imagine we can use all the help we can get."

"Morgaine?" Alex was calling from the side door. I'd given him a key to let himself back in when he'd finished getting ready. Lingus and I both stood and walked toward the shop. The birds who'd joined us at the fountain tittered and flew off into the bushes.

"We're here!" We rounded the corner and Alex stepped aside and held the door for us. Lingus hesitated only a moment before coming in. He was clearly not comfortable in human habitats. The three of us climbed back up to my flat in silence, resolved to begin our work in trying to find the demon again. Pip was waiting near the door to greet us. The four of us walked to the back room, Pip taking up his watch in the reading chair, while Alex helped me prepare the circle.

Chapter Four

Hours later, we stopped for lunch. Lingus left through the window, his translucent wings sparkling like the finest glitter as they unfurled to carry him away. We were still no closer to finding the demon, although Lingus had marked even more minor demons for us. The only thing left to do was to search further afield. This included all bodies of water nearby - the sea, rivers, and inland waterway. Lingus seemed to think that even with sufficient protection wards, as well as his presence, I still shouldn't join the search party. If the demon got a sense of me, and it was strong enough, it might be able to use my tracking spell against me. But, if it sensed the magic when Alex and Lingus got near, I would be far enough removed from it to remain undetected.

I was making sandwiches for us when the phone rang. I could tell from the tingling at the base of my neck that it was Brighid before I answered (well, that and the dedicated ring-tone). "Hey, chick!"

"Hey! I passed by the store earlier and saw your sign. What gives? You OK?"

Think fast, I told myself. "Yeah, yeah…I'm just taking a few days off. Been feeling a bit drained lately, and I think the party was the last straw. I just need a few days to recuperate."

I swear I could hear her eyes narrowing over the phone. "You're having a dirty weekend with Alex, aren't you?!"

I looked over and saw Alex watching from his seat at the table, where he patiently awaited his lunch. I dashed down the hall to my bedroom and shut the door. "No, I am not." Knowing she couldn't see me, I trusted in her ability to pick up on the humor in my tone as I solemnly laid a hand across my heart, fluttered my lashes with doe-like innocence, and said in my best Scarlett O'Hara voice, "Although I will be seeing him, I promise you that my virtue shall remain intact."

She laughed out loud at that. "Oh, please - your virtue hasn't been intact since the 1990s! But, OK, Mora. Whatever you say."

"I really am just a bit drained. I haven't had a vacation in ages, you know." All of that was true. Just because I was drained from exhaustively searching for a demon…

Brighid seemed placated and after a few minutes of idle chit-chat, we hung up. I headed back into the kitchen to finish up our lunch. Alex watched me walk back in with eyebrows raised. "That seemed intense. Everything all right?"

"Yeah, just my friend, Brighid - the red-head from the Halloween party?" I said, thinking maybe he'd seen her when he did his kettle-filling disappearing act. He nodded. "She has a tendency to over-react to things…" I stopped and met his eyes. "Actually, I have a confession to make."

"Another one? You're just full of secrets, Miss Clemenson," he said, a smile quirking up the corners of his mouth. "Okay…" he gestured for me to continue.

There was nothing for it, so I just blurted it out. "I had to tell Brighid something to explain your presence, and I said I was helping you research the maritime history of the area, but she thinks we've just started dating, and I let her believe that."

"That…that's as good a cover as any," he was annoyingly accommodating, and his smile, while not actually mocking, was cutely infuriating. "I shall be honored to pretend to court you, my dear."

"Cheeky monkey." I turned back to the sandwiches to hide my blushing - I could feel the heat of it, and the sound of his chuckling just intensified it. I didn't know what was wrong with me. I wasn't the sort to let anyone fluster me, but something about the way Alex looked at me was disarming. A few deep breaths later, I carried the plates to the table. He was still grinning. I set the plate down in front of him and he winked at me. This time there was no escape to hide my blush, so I sat down across from him with as much dignity as I could muster and ate my sandwich.

After lunch, I set about fashioning a talisman for Alex to carry when he and Lingus went out on their hunt later.

"Hey," I said to Alex, "take out that ribbon." He'd continued to wear his hair tied back these last couple of days. It suited him, although he looked really nice with it loose as well.

"What? Why?" He asked, but pulled the ribbon out anyway.

"It's for the talisman." I took my scissors and, gently reaching underneath to the base of his skull, I snipped a small tuft of hair. He shuddered. "What's wrong? I didn't hurt you did I?"

"No, not at all," he said. "It just tickled." He gave me… was that a *shy* smile? He took my free hand. "You've got such soft hands," he said.

I snatched my hand away and playfully swatted his shoulder. "Are you teasing me? Don't make me regret letting Brighid think you're boyfriend material."

His eyes widened and his brows shot up. "No, I…" he cleared his throat and took on a serious expression, gesturing to the scissors and hair in my hand and said "carry on." There was still the ghost of a smile on his lips, though. I couldn't decide if he was teasing, or really flirting.

I shook my head and reached up to snip a tuft of my own hair.

I began braiding together strands of my hair with his and a thin chain made of iron while intoning a protective ward.

"Are you sure that's not a love talisman?" Alex said with a smirk.

I gave him the stink-eye. That was definitely teasing. "I know it looks like it, but go with me on this. Braiding our hair together with the chain will act as protection for you."

Wrapping the braid around the base of the pendulum we'd been using in our tracking attempts, I fastened it securely using a strand of fabric from Lingus' tunic that I'd collected earlier. "Now I'm binding the tracking spell I created to this braided talisman, and using this fabric from Lingus will combine his protection with mine to help keep you, and the spell within the pendulum, safe from harm."

The lads were planning to go out at sundown, when it was more likely the demon would be active. If it were still especially weak, it might not move far from its hiding place, but it would need to come out to gather whatever sustenance it could to help rebuild its strength.

I found some quiet time that afternoon to cuddle with Pip. There are few things more soothing than the warmth of a purring cat in your lap. Pip seemed to have enjoyed our alone time, too. He'd been, in his own kitty way, just as harried as we'd been by recent events. It was a nice bit of respite, and I treasured it, knowing that things were going to get weird sooner rather than later. I left Pip reluctantly. It was time to see Alex and Lingus off on their task. Lingus was waiting for us in the garden when we went down.

"You have prepared?" he asked.

I held up the talisman-infused pendulum. "This has a protective ward, as well as the tracking spell imbued within it." I handed it and the map to Alex. "Please be careful. And call me if you need anything." While I'd been having my quiet time with Pip, Alex had been out shopping for a pay as you go phone so we could stay in touch while they were out looking for the demon. Since I keep the fence's gate locked most of the time, it was easiest just to let them out through the front of the building. As we made our way through the shop floor to the front exit, I noticed Lingus seemed to be fascinated by the array of items in the shop. After seeing Alex and Lingus out, I closed and locked the door behind them. At a bit of a loss at first as to what to do while they were gone, I eventually settled on doing a meditation. At least I could focus on something other than fretting over what was going on beyond my four walls.

It was such a lovely, mild night that I decided to do my meditation in the garden. I visualized a simple protective dome around me, calmed my breathing, cleared my thoughts and opened my mind. Sometimes I got flashes of images that related to anything going on in my life that had been troubling me. These images were usually of things or people that would help me overcome whatever obstacle had presented itself. Tonight, there were a few fleeting images of Alex standing before me, blocking some unseen threat. I also got flashes of Lingus, a kind expression on his face, speaking in the lilting tones of his native language. Nothing that gave me any clear idea of the direction of events. But then, these weren't precognitive images. I had occasionally experienced precognitive dreams, but never had precognitive meditations. I refocused myself, and concentrated on sending protective energy out to Alex and Lingus. I imagined them standing before me, each surrounded by a translucent opalescent bubble that deflected anything harmful directed at them. "As I will, so mote it be."

After bringing my thoughts back to the present time and space, I released my visualized protective dome, took several deep breaths, and opened my eyes. I was not alone. Seated across from me, well outside of where my protective dome had been was another creature like Lingus. This one appeared younger, blond hair curling softly around its shoulders, blue eyes instead of green, but wearing the same type of clothing. One exception to its appearance was the presence of tiny horns, like the buds of a young deer's antlers, on its head. Startled, a shout caught in my throat. Maybe the fact that I was calmed from my meditation, and that the creature bore enough of a resemblance to Lingus to be of the same species, kept me from screaming. Still, it was a bit disconcerting to open my eyes to find it sat staring at me.

It smiled and bowed its head. "Greetings. I am Adaine." This creature was also male, with slightly accented English, like Lingus. "I am a guardian of the wildlands and its inhabitants. I have heeded the call of my kinsman Lingus to assist."

Well, okay then. "Hello, Adaine. I am Morgaine. Thank you for coming. I was about to go in and make myself a cup of tea."

"No need to invite me in," he said, before I'd even had a chance to offer. "I prefer to remain out of doors."

"Ah, of course. I can wait for a bit. Um…Lingus and my friend Alex have gone to see if they can find the demon. They've been gone…" I reached over to where I'd left my watch before beginning my meditation and peered at it, surprised at how much time had passed since I'd started my meditation. "Wow, they've been gone a little over an hour now. I'm guessing they haven't found the demon yet."

"I am sure they will succeed," Adaine said. "I am unsure of what I can do to assist at this moment, but no doubt Lingus will be able to find a use for me."

He was…polite, this one, but in a different way than Lingus. Where Lingus seemed to be kind as a matter of course, Adaine seemed to be kind because it was expected. Almost like a rowdy child on his best behavior. I suspected this Daemon was an even wilder variety than Lingus. I gestured around us. "You are welcome to remain in the garden, if you like. Lingus is making a temporary home here. If there is anything I can get for you, just let me know. Lingus seems to manage his own meals, but if there is anything in my kitchen that you would like, you need only ask."

"That is very kind of you, Morgaine, but I shall provide my own sustenance as well."

The moon, still full and bright, was high in the sky and therefore the garden was very well lit. Adaine and I sat in silence a while, the only sounds those of the sea breeze and a few late-season crickets. "It really is a lovely night," I said.

"Indeed. I sense a fox nearby. The full moon will be of great help as he hunts his dinner."

"Foxes are part of your domain, then?" Adaine nodded. "I know Lingus seems to be attuned with birds."

"Yes. Lingus' domain includes small creatures such as birds and squirrels. Mine includes foxes, deer, wolves, and the like."

"Until yesterday, I had no knowledge of the existence of nature guardians. I've always welcomed the idea of the Fae, but never expected to be sitting in my garden having a conversation with one."

Adaine smiled. "While I suppose you could say we are of the Fae, faeries as humans understand them are a different species."

Wait, what? Actual faeries are real, too? It seems obvious that witches would believe in all sorts of faerie tales and the creatures within them, but actually, most of us are pretty practical about that sort of thing, and view them more as archetypes than actual existing entities.

"Very few humans are ever allowed to see us, Adaine continued, "let alone get close enough for conversation. We rarely emerge from our domains in any event. But we observe the passage of time, the comings and goings of species, the help and the hindrance of humankind." I thought I sensed a particular emphasis on the word "hindrance", something about the way his mouth formed the word, but it might have been my imagination.

It was a bit unsettling, knowing that we're always watched by guardians of the natural world. I was tempted to ask Adaine about the nature guardians' views on mankind's stewardship of the earth, if they planned to counteract the planetary warming effects in any way. But I wasn't sure I wanted to know if a war against humankind waged by the protectors of nature was imminent. "Do your kind live long - if that's not an impertinent question?"

"We can live many centuries, yes. Some have existed for millennia."

I checked my watch again. I was trying not to worry, but I wished they'd at least call me with an update. I could have called them I suppose, but if they were in the middle of the demon's lair, that could really ruin the day. "Adaine, I have some tasks to attend to. Will you be alright if I leave you?"

"Of course. If you have need of me, simply speak my name."

Lingus had said much the same thing. Man, I really hoped they could only hear their names and not other conversations. I went back in through the side door and headed up the stairs. Pip was pacing in the kitchen. He seemed agitated, but I couldn't work out why, unless he was just picking up on my vaguely concealed jitters. Despite the meditation, I was still not completely at ease.

I made a cup of tea and carried it to the ritual space to continue my search for an appropriately adaptable spell. I kept a notebook and pencil in a pocket on the chair, and got them out to make some notes. Flipping through the pages, I made notes from the spells I'd bookmarked earlier, and searched for something - anything - that could be used for a trapping spell. When I started getting a headache, I put the book down and concentrated on my notes. Using a fresh sheet of paper, I fashioned what had to be the strongest protection ward I could possibly make from my notes. It was a personal ward, meaning I could use it for myself, but to apply it to another person would require their knowledge, consent, and actual physical presence. When Alex and Lingus returned, I could ward them. Adaine, too, if he wished it. In the meanwhile, I set about warding myself with my new spell.

The effect was astonishing. Once I'd intoned the words, a visible glow emanated from my body, formed a bubble around me and then disappeared with a 'pop'. The protection was absolutely still there, I could feel it zinging about me, but the visible glow was gone. Whether it would be strong enough to protect me from the demon was yet to be seen. I tried a modified version on Pip, after explaining what I was about to do, and trusting that he understood. The fact he didn't run away I took as his consent. The same glow and pop and, bless him, his fur stood on end as the protection zinged around him and finally settled. Goodness, the look he gave me. He knew he was OK, and I am sure he understood the purpose, but he wasn't particularly thrilled with the static-y results.

I checked my watch again. Time seemed to be dragging. It was thoroughly dark now, and this was probably the best time for them to find the demon. Also the most dangerous, as it might be fully active, even if it was still weakened. I paced a bit. Then sat and searched spells again. This time I found some good candidates. Sometimes you have to put something aside for a while and look again later with fresh eyes. I made notes. There was not enough to form a complete spell, yet, but it was a start at least. I paced some more. I searched spells some more.

Finally, I flopped down on my bed, grabbed my phone and dialed my friend Whither, who had a metaphysical shop of her own a few states away, but left the running of it to employees to travel around the east coast, collecting mushrooms, herbs, and other magical flora. The phone rang several times before Whither answered, which suggested she'd been driving and had to find a safe place to pull over. I made some small-talk and then asked her if she could overnight some specific spell ingredients that I didn't have. If anyone would have the most obscure plants, herbs, powders, or elements, it would be Whither. She was discreet enough not to ask what I needed them for, but I could tell her interest was piqued.

After we hung up, I paced some more. Then, I settled in the living room and stared at the clock. The later it got, the more jittery I got. Eventually I sat quietly, eyes closed, focusing on my breathing. After a while, Pip joined me. The waiting was becoming excruciating! The next time those boys went out without me, I was going to insist they call and check in at least once an hour.

I'd drifted off into an uneasy doze, with Pip curled at my side. When the phone did finally ring, we both jumped. I grabbed the receiver and said "Hello?" a little louder than I'd intended.

"It's Alex."

"For f@#'s sake, it's about bloody time!"* I didn't say. What I did say, with more calm than I felt, was, "Any luck?"

"Well...yes. Perhaps too much luck."

The hell was that supposed to mean? "Are you all right?"

"Yes, we're fine. And, we've located the demon. The good news is that Lingus senses it is still fairly weak. However, it is gaining strength more quickly than we would like. We need to act fast. Have you managed a trapping spell?"

"No, but I did come up with a really good protection ward, and I have some solid notes toward fashioning a trap."

"Good, good." Alex said, and paused. I heard Lingus clear his throat in the background.

"Alex?..." I prompted.

"You must tell her." I heard Lingus say.

"Tell me what? Alex, what's going on?"

"Well, as I said, the good news is it is still weak…"

"Aaaaand? What's the bad news?"

Alex was waffling. I heard a rustling sound and then Lingus' voice came over the line.

"Morgaine, we have determined what sort of demon we are dealing with. It is a high-level incubus."

"One of those things that seduces people in their sleep?"

"Yes, the female is the succubus."

I nodded, even though Lingus could not see me. "Yeah, I've heard of them. Are they especially difficult to deal with?"

"Normally, they never enter the physical plane. They are dream demons. The fact that this one is made flesh and walking the earth is concerning, yes. But, that's not the worst part."

"And the worst part would be?"

Lingus hesitated. Another rustle and Alex was back.

"The worst part," he said, then fumbled his words again. *Pull it together Ramsey,* I thought. "We've found it in a bar and...grille." He pronounced the 'e' on the end of grille - 'grill-y'. It would be cute if I weren't so frustrated I wanted to reach through the phone and shake him. "The worst part is that he is attempting to seduce Brighid. And she seems to be falling under his spell."

Goddess defend. That woman and her hormones. "Can't you...I don't know, go break it up - pretend to be a jealous boyfriend?"

"No, the demon would feed off of that energy, even if it was pretended."

"A protective big-brother, then?"

"Again, any emotional energy will only feed the creature - Brighid doesn't know me by sight, and would likely not just play along. Her reaction of confusion, even anger -"

"Would feed the demon." I finished.

Lingus had been listening in. "I am afraid we require your magical skills, Morgaine. And, I regret that it is likely to put you in some danger."

Alex chimed in with "I wish you'd finished the trap."

"Yeah, well, you try coming up with a spell that's never been invented to trap something you know nothing about, skippy!"

"I thought 'skippy' was a friendly nickname. That didn't sound very fri-"

"NOT NOW!" I snapped. "I'm on my way." I put the phone down and looked at Pip. "It is, it would seem, on now." He mewed sympathetically. How I wish I'd been able to get that protective amulet made for Brighid.

I dashed about, collecting everything I could think of that might assist me in getting Brighid away from the demon. It was obviously feeding on the desire it had sparked in her. I hated to think how much stronger it could get if they actually…if she…I just couldn't even think about it. I would have to think of something on the way. The worry was that if I got too close, it could all fall apart and we could lose the battle before it had even begun. And, Alex couldn't approach either - even if his accent gave him away as my new friend, she would not react well to the interruption, and that would feed the bloody demon. There was a misdirection element to my protection ward, but would it be enough?

I had a sudden flash of inspiration. Grabbing my phone, I dialed her mobile number. It went to voice-mail. Not only did it go to voice-mail, it went as soon as the number connected, without ringing. That meant she likely had turned the phone off…or that something was preventing her from receiving calls. Could the demon be strong enough to do that already? So much for the easy way out of this.

I headed down the stairs and out into the garden. Adaine appeared almost as soon as his name left my lips. I told him what was happening. "I'm going there now to meet them. You are welcome to come, although at this point, I don't know what any of us can do."

He nodded. "I shall accompany you. You will think of something. Try to calm your thoughts as we travel."

He sounded more sure of me than I felt, that was for certain. But, I did as he said and calmed my thoughts as best as I could. We walked in silence to the little alley between shops where the parking lot was. As I started to get into the car, I noticed Adaine hesitating. "I'm a good driver, I promise."

"I'm sure. But…I am not comfortable being confined within man-made structures."

"Well, it's too far to walk quickly, and time is of the essence."

"Yes, of course," he said. "But I have my own means of travel. If you can tell me where to go, I shall meet you there."

I did my best to give him directions on how to get to the Salt Air. He seemed to understand my jumbled instructions and floated off in the general direction of the place. I got in the car and drove, faster than I should have, but not quite fast enough to be dangerous or attract attention.

Oh, Brighid, you silly girl.

What was she thinking? For that matter, how much of her thinking was hers, and how much was being controlled by this demon? If she were wearing any of her protective pendants, this demon was obviously not affected by them, but then, that was one of the lessons of witchcraft that I'd had the most trouble getting Brighid to follow - the need to always have some sort of protection about you.

I turned a corner a little faster than intended and the screech of my wheels broke me out of my reverie. Instead of mentally admonishing my friend for likely not wearing her protective pendants, I should be focusing on how to get her out of this mess. If I got her back unharmed, I would tell her everything - the truth about Alex, the demon incursion, time travel, everything - and make her go stay with her mother for safety.

Brighid's home was on the way to the Salt Air. We had sets of each other's keys, and I used mine to let myself in. Quickly as I could, I ran to her room and pulled a couple of strands of her hair from her brush. A plan was starting to percolate in my mind. I was thinking of a spell I could use that would utilize the strands of Brighid's hair. It was a spell that would normally be against my morals to use as it would cause some physical discomfort, but it was harmless overall and given the dire circumstances, I was willing to tempt having fate boomeranging on me by using it. I was fairly confident Brighid would forgive me. I ran back out to the car and got back on the road, driving as fast as possible without drawing attention to myself. My nerves were raw. I knew I needed to calm down. I forced myself to take deep breaths. The calmer I could be, the more help to Brighid I would be.

At last, I pulled into the parking lot of the Salt Air Bar and Grille. It had been less than ten minutes, even with the stop at Brighid's, but had seemed to take forever. Alex and Lingus were standing in a blind spot between some shrubs and the dumpsters. The Mexican petunias, or "purple showers" had dropped their daily blossoms, but the confectionery-colored pink and yellow Lantanas glowed in the moonlight. If it weren't for Alex's height, I wouldn't have seen them right away - the Lantanas were almost as tall as Lingus and nearly obscured him completely. I made my way over to them, trying to glimpse into the bar. I couldn't see Brighid. I hoped I wasn't too late. When I got to where Alex and Lingus were, I noticed that Adaine had already found them.

"Where is she? Am I too late?" I tried to squash the panic, but the feeling still attempted to bubble its way up through my guts.

Alex pulled me into the blind spot and held my hand tightly. "No, they are still in there. We can't see them because they are on the dance floor on the other side of the bar. But from here, we can see all exits, and they haven't come out."

I breathed a sigh of relief.

"We don't have much time, though. Have you had any ideas?"

"Perhaps if we go in together," I suggested, "pretend to be on a date, we can fashion some sort of escape."

Alex nodded. "But, we will need your magic to misdirect the demon. We need to remain as anonymous to him as possible."

"A glamour," Lingus said.

"Precisely," I nodded. As a plan began to form, my confidence started returning. "Keep watch - I am going to fashion a charm that will make her think she feels ill and that should get her to go to the ladies room. If I can get close enough to her to get it in a pocket or something, once it takes effect I can follow her to the toilets and can reveal myself to her."

Lingus nodded, "And somehow convince her to leave with you - without her suitor."

"That's going to be the tricky part. I can only hope his influence over her diminishes if she isn't in his presence."

Even a glamour wouldn't hide the fact that I was a witch if the demon was strong enough to sense it. He just wouldn't know what I really looked like and if I got us out of this, that might buy us some time. I could only hope that he wouldn't have been able to sense Brighid was a witch - since she wasn't a hereditary witch, maybe she'd be missing some hereditary marker. Or something. In any event. it looked like I was going to get to test the effectiveness of my new protection ward whether I was ready or not.

Chapter Five

Deep breaths. I kept making myself take deep breaths. Meanwhile, Alex continued to hold my hand, and gently stroked my forearm while whispering affirmations. "You are strong. You can do this." That sort of thing. I normally consider myself a pretty confident, forward person. I usually don't rattle easily, but then, I don't have to come face to face with actual high-ranking demons on a regular basis. Or at all, actually. Despite knowing what I needed to do, and trusting my magic, I was still fighting nerves. Alex seemed to be willing some of his strength into me, and I smiled my appreciation at him.

Nearby, Lingus and Adaine were engaged in quiet conversation. Once I felt calmer, I began concentrating on crafting our glamour. When I felt ready, Alex and I joined hands. I envisioned my protective dome around both of us and began the incantation for my glamour. I could tell it was working when I felt a tingling on my skin. Alex's fingers twitched slightly, which I took as a sign that he felt it too. When I was done, we turned to Lingus and Adaine.

They both smiled, and Lingus nodded, "It is perfect." I kept it fairly simple, changing our hair color and length, and eye color. I gave Alex short blonde hair and grey eyes, and I went with curly black hair, darkening my naturally greenish eyes to a deep brown. Anything more elaborate - changing body shapes or height - would have required a potion and more intensive spell.

It was time.

"Adaine and I will channel our own powers to strengthen your glamour," Lingus said. That would certainly help in case my nerves got the better of me and it started to slip. I could only hope now that the protections I'd used for Alex, and my own newly created personal protection ward would be enough to keep us from drawing any attention from the incubus. We walked, holding hands, to the door where we paused to try to find Brighid.

"There she is," Alex said. She was still on the dance floor, twirling and gyrating and laughing with abandon. With her was…

"Oh my, he is stunning," I whispered. I felt my grip on Alex's hand loosen as I stared. He was tall, with close-cut wavy dark brown hair. His eyes were so piercingly blue they fairly glowed. He was the most exquisite creature…at that point I felt Alex squeeze my hand.

"Morgaine…" Alex said, gently but firmly.

Creature…yes, creature, I thought. I mustn't forget what we were dealing with. He was certainly made to seduce. I shook off the enchantment and scanned the rest of the room. Other women (and a couple of men) were also staring at him, enraptured. Predictably, there were a handful of men and women who looked at him with either jealousy or admiration.

I took another deep breath and we stepped through the door. We made our way to a corner table near the dance floor. Brighid and the incubus seemed tireless, keeping up their dance into the next song. A waiter breezed by and asked for our drinks order. I asked for red wine and Alex straight whiskey.

I leaned forward. "Brighid's wearing her tunic with the huge pockets in it. If I can get close enough to her, I might be able to drop the charm into one of them."

Alex got my plan straight away, and smiled. He held out his hand. "May I have this dance?" As we stood, he dropped some cash on the table to cover our drinks.

We made our way to the dance floor, starting on the perimeter, so as not to draw Brighid's and the incubus' attention by just shimmying right up to them. As the song progressed, we eased closer and closer until we were within a foot of them. And then the song ended. I froze. I needed us to be moving to cover my motion of slipping the charm into Brighid's pocket. What if they walked off? Alex and I locked eyes and I held my breath. His grip tightened around my waist. Brighid and the incubus were standing close together, foreheads nearly touching. He was saying something and she was laughing. Then another song started. He grabbed her, spun her once, and dipped her. Her laughter was free and unselfconscious. I couldn't remember when I had last seen my friend so happy in the company of a man. It nearly broke my heart that I was going to have to put an end to her euphoria.

Relieved, Alex and I began dancing again, inching ever closer. We moved into position just behind and slightly to the side of Brighid. I guided Alex between me and Brighid, my plan being to fake a hug in order to lean forward and drop the charm into her pocket. It was all going according to plan. More people had moved out to the dance floor, making it easier to press close to Brighid without seeming to be invading her personal space. Taking advantage of the crush of bodies, I leaned into Alex and reached my hand forward as he curled into me and feigned nuzzling my neck. When I brushed the fabric of Brighid's tunic pocket, I gently pushed the pocket open to drop in the charm. I felt it slide against the fabric and into the pocket. I gave Alex a pat on the back to indicate success and we allowed the press of the crowd to move us a few inches over, away from Brighid and the incubus. We were still close enough to keep an eye on them, and I cast glances over at every opportunity to observe Brighid. As I'd hoped, she started slowing a bit. I saw her put one hand to her head and the other on her belly. She leaned forward and said something to the incubus, then turned and headed in the direction of the toilets.

Alex nodded. I made to turn to follow Brighid. Just then I felt a hand close around my wrist. Again, I froze. Alex saw the panic in my eyes and looked up.

"Hello, friends!" It was the incubus. He was dancing in front of us then. "I seem to have temporarily lost my partner. Mind if I join you?" He had an English accent. Because of course he did. Brighid loves an accent.

Amazingly, Alex and I managed to keep moving. I was fighting panic, now. The last thing we'd wanted was to draw the incubus' attention. I hoped Lingus' and Adaine's strengthening of my glamour was working, because I didn't know how long it would hold, otherwise. We continued dancing, Alex and I fiercely trying to look as if we were having a good time, the incubus still holding my wrist, gyrating on the other side of me.

"I'm Ian," the incubus shouted over the music.

"Oh…um, I'm Lisa," I said - it was the first name to pop into my head.

"Tom," Alex said with a manly nod.

The incubus…or, "Ian", dropped his grip to my hand and spun me around, away from Alex, then pulled me in closer to him. "Mmm," he said, narrowing his eyes and making as if to sniff me. "You're delectable!"

Alex reached around, grabbed my free hand and gathered me to him, pulling me in close and trying to pivot me away from the incubus. Ian released me, thankfully. I put my arms around Alex's waist and held on tightly. Ian slithered around behind me and placed his hands on my hips. Just like that, we were a dancing Morgaine sandwich. Alex and I kept our smiles plastered upon our faces, struggling to keep them as authentic looking as possible. My mind was racing. I was desperate to find a way to extricate myself and go to Brighid, but reluctant to leave Alex to the mercy of the incubus. I was afraid if Alex had to speak too much, his accent would be noted by the incubus, and that could cause more issues. "Ian" might want to bond over nationality or something.

I couldn't believe our luck when a brash blonde in a tube top, push-up bra, and mini skirt twirled her way over to us, and pressed her writhing body against Ian. I was even more relieved when his attention was immediately drawn to her and he dropped his hands from my hips. Physically, the demon was as hale as any human male, but the fact that he was so easily distracted suggested that he was still in a weakened state insofar as his powers went. Alex and I took the opportunity to dance away from him as quickly as we could. We made our way to a pillar near the edge of the dance floor and slipped behind it. I held on to Alex for a moment, willing my trembling to stop. He held me close and I could feel his heart beating, fast and strenuously. I looked up. Our eyes met, and I felt a calmness steal over me. I needed to make a move. With any luck, Brighid would still be in the toilets.

"I'm sorry I didn't make a stronger attempt to get you away - I just...I didn't want to give him any emotion to feed on."

"It's OK," I said. "The last thing we needed was to have a big scene."

Alex gave me a tight smile. "Go. I'll keep an eye on things out here."

I nodded and headed toward the toilets, casting a glance back to see the incubus still dancing with the blond. He seemed just as into her as he had seemed with Brighid. I eased the door to the toilets open and slipped inside. Brighid was alone and leaning over one of the sinks, splashing her face with cool water. I sidled up to her, slipped my hand into her pocket and extracted the charm. She looked up and caught my eye in the wall to wall, sinks to ceiling mirror.

Her brow furrowed. "Who…?"

I took a deep breath and sighed, releasing the glamour.

"Mora?" She stood and faced me. "What are you doing here? And, why the glamour?"

"Brighid, it's very important that you listen to me, and trust me."

She seemed not to have heard me. "Never mind - I'm glad you're here," she smiled and hopped up and down, all effects of the charm seemingly gone now. "I met someone! Oh, Mora - he's PERFECT!"

"No, Brighid, he's not-"

"And, he's English, too! You didn't tell me Alex had a friend with him!"

It felt like my heart dropped into my stomach. "Is that what he told you? That he's a friend of Alex?"

"Huh? No...I just assumed. I was going to ask-"

I breathed a sigh of relief at that. If she'd already mentioned Alex to the incubus, things could have got really sticky.

"Mora? What's going on?"

I took her face in my hands and looked her in the eye. "Brighid, you have to trust me. We need to leave. Now."

"What?" she shook my hands off. "I can't leave - I just found this guy!"

"You didn't find him, he found you."

"So?" She beamed again. "He's gorgeous! Just wait til you meet him!"

"Brighid," I said, perhaps more sternly than I'd intended. I had no idea how much sway the incubus held over Brighid's emotions. "I HAVE met him. He is not who he seems."

I could see her struggling to process my words and her own impressions. I hoped she trusted me enough to know I was only looking out for her.

She frowned at me. "Mora, what are you doing? Are you trying to ruin this for me?"

"Brighid, no." I grabbed her hands. "I promise you I will explain everything, but we are not safe here. YOU are not safe."

She started to shake her head, confusion stealing into her expression. Maybe distance from the incubus meant his hold on her was lessening.

"Please, just come with me." I had to get through to her. "Come back to my place. I need to show you something. And then, I promise, if you want to come back and find your guy, I'll drive you back myself."

"At least let me say goodbye," she moved toward the door and I tightened my grip on her hands.

"No. Trust me - he's not going anywhere for a while."

She looked me in the eye, then nodded. "OK. But we're coming straight back here - you promised."

"Yes," I said, relief flooding through me. "Now let's go. Quickly."

I opened the door and checked that the coast was clear. I turned back to Brighid and held up a finger. I took another deep breath and sighed again, renewing the glamour.

"S'good look for you, Mora."

I clasped her hand and led us down the corridor. We paused at the end and I scanned the room for Alex and the incubus. Thankfully, both were where I'd left them. I caught Alex's eye and nodded. He made his way toward us as I pulled Brighid after me, moving to the right toward the door. I was hoping to get her past the open view of the dance floor and on the other side of the central bar before she noticed-

"What. The. Hell?!" Brighid stood still, watching "Ian" and the blond cavorting on the dance floor. A number of other women were circling, looking for an opening. Suddenly, the grip of his influence over Brighid took hold again and she moved to go toward him. I fought to keep my grip on her hand and cast Alex a desperate look. He noticed the trouble, and jumped into action. As Brighid opened her mouth wide to shout at the incubus, Alex swept a clean linen napkin off a nearby table, took two quick strides toward us and stuffed the napkin in Brighid's mouth. The shock of that was enough to break her concentration on the dance floor, and she looked at me and reached toward the napkin with her free hand. Alex grabbed her hand before she could remove the napkin and we quickly made our way, half-dragging Brighid, to the door.

We didn't let up our pace until we got to my car and shoved Brighid into it. She sat, napkin still in place and looked furiously from one to the other of us. Lingus and Adaine approached from the blind spot. Brighid's eyes grew wide when she saw them. I looked at Alex. "We gotta go."

Lingus unfurled his translucent wings, and Adaine did the same. "Adaine and I will return to your garden, as soon as you are safely on your way."

Alex jumped in the back seat. I got into the driver's seat, started the car and headed back to my place. I hoped the incubus hadn't noticed any of the confusion. Our best chance was if he was still fawning over the busty blonde. I checked the rear-view mirror. The coast seemed clear. Brighid managed to recover herself enough to finally pluck the napkin from her mouth. She turned in her seat to glare at me.

"What. The. Hell. IS GOING ON?!" She was furious.

"Brighid, calm down. I'll explain everything."

"What was Ian doing with that...that...floozy?!" I nearly laughed then, 'floozy' was not a word I would expect Brighid to use.

Alex leaned forward. "Being a cad."

Brighid whipped her head around and shared the glare with him. "And just who the hell are you?"

I released the glamour. Alex resumed his normal appearance. He reached over the seat to offer his hand. "Alex Ramsey. Pleased to make your acquaintance."

Brighid's eyes flickered down to Alex's hand, but she didn't take it. "You're the military guy." She looked back at me. "I don't know what is going on, but I'm not speaking to you." She folded her arms across her chest and stared forward.

"Brighid," I began. "I was trying to warn you-"

"Nope," she put her fingers in her ears. "La la la la, I can't heeearrr you."

I rolled my eyes and concentrated on driving. Might as well let her stew for a while. The further from the incubus we got, the more likely she'd come around as the strength of his enchantment waned. Alex caught my eye in the rear view mirror. I just shrugged.

An hour later, we sat out on the garden patio. I'd managed to get Brighid to accept a cup of tea. It had grown quite cool out, so I'd wrapped her in a blanket and put on my own fleece jacket. She sat staring with a mixture of curiosity and alarm at Lingus and Adaine, who seemed not to mind the intense attention. They sat on the ground just past the concrete of the patio, silently waiting. Brighid had yet to speak to us. I think she was probably in shock, and I couldn't blame her. We'd explained what was going on as best as we could. What I wasn't sure of, was how much of "Ian's" influence might still have hold of her.

"Brighid, please," I sat beside her on the lounge and put my hand on her arm. "Say something."

Finally she turned her gaze to me. Confusion, anger, hurt. It was all there in her eyes. She sighed. "Mora...I don't understand what's happening."

"I know sweetie," I pulled her into a tight hug, nearly causing her to spill her tea. "It's a lot to take in. How are you feeling?"

She sat up straight and took a deep breath. "Physically? Exhausted. Emotionally? I don't know - confused mostly, I think. I'm...I'm kind of numb."

"I shouldn't wonder," Alex said. "It's not every day one nearly gets entrapped by an incubus."

Brighid glowered at him. That was a good sign, I thought.

"Speaking of traps," I said, "I've asked a friend to overnight some things to me. I think I might be onto something. I just need to consult some texts." I'd been giving some thought to my notes since we'd left the bar. Now that we knew we were dealing with an incubus, I thought I might be able to pull from other spells to craft a trap. I'd asked Whither for things I didn't sell in the store. Herbs that could be toxic if mishandled, powdered substances that were common in dark workings, and less common to the average witch's inventory. I'd also asked to borrow a manuscript she'd acquired in her travels, and I was hopeful I could find information to help me bridge the gap between what I *could* do, and what I *needed* to do. Whither didn't provide these things to just anyone. She knew me well enough to understand that if I was asking for them, they were for an important purpose, and that I did not take their powers lightly. "The things I've asked my friend to send should cover just about any type of spell I can think of."

"I want to help," Brighid said with determination as she leaned forward and set her empty teacup on the table.

"No!" I, Alex, and Lingus said in unison. Adaine was staying out of it.

She looked around at us fiercely. "What do you mean 'no'?! It was me that incubus nearly had!"

"Exactly," I said. "You've been through enough."

She stared at me. "Dammit, Mora. You don't think I'm good enough, do you?"

"No, that's not it. It isn't about talent, Brighid. It's more to do with experience. I was born to this, you are still learning." Brighid's insecurity wasn't entirely out of character, but it seemed to be a bit in overdrive at the moment. I decided to attribute it to the shock of what had happened this evening. But, I didn't want to seem to be talking down to her. "You have plenty of aptitude, just not as much practical experience."

She didn't look entirely convinced. "Well, how am I supposed to improve my skill - how am I supposed to gain experience - if you won't let me?!"

"My dear," Lingus had moved silently to her side, she jumped when he spoke, "your friend only wishes to protect you. If she is worrying about you during the working, it could cause her a mistake, and all could be lost."

Brighid stared at him, before turning to look at Alex and then at me. "But that's just it. I want to help because I don't want anything to happen to you, Mora. I would do anything to keep you safe."

"Oh, sweetie," I clasped her hand, "the knowledge that you are safe is the best help you could give me." I thought I was getting through to her.

She chewed her lip briefly. "OK. But I want you to promise me that if you can see any other way I can DO something, you will let me."

I nodded. "That's fair enough. Now, come on, let's go in." I wanted her to stay here tonight, I didn't think I could bear not to have my friend close after so nearly losing her. "We're all exhausted and it's after midnight."

Alex stood and started gathering the dishes. "The incubus will likely go to ground for the day. We should sleep for a bit, and then get back to work."

"Adaine and I will return to the bar," Lingus said. "We will attempt to trail the demon to its hiding place. Sleep well, my friends." With that, he and Adaine drifted off back toward the bar.

Chapter Six

Alex stayed on the sofa-bed again. He'd actually packed an overnight bag when he'd been at his hotel earlier and brought it back, rightly thinking it might prove to be another late night here.

Brighid and I shared my bed, lying face to face and holding hands like we used to do at sleepovers when we were younger. Pip was rolled into a ball between our bellies. I smiled at Brighid. "Leave it to you to find the perfect man, and he turns out to be a demon."

It was good to see her smile. "Yeah, just my damn luck. He was hot though, wasn't he?"

"Ohhh, indeed he was. I shudder to think what he might *actually* look like, however."

"Ewwww." We laughed although there was little mirth in it, mostly it was a release of tension. We were silent for a while, Brighid twirling my moonstone ring around my finger, thinking. Then she looked me in the eye. "What are you going to do?"

I heaved a big sigh. "I have no idea. I hope that between my notes and Whither's care package I can cobble something together."

"Will you at least let me help you with that? Even if you banish me from the working itself?"

I smiled and pulled her into a hug, Pip half-heartedly protested at getting squished between us. "Sure thing. I'd like that." We eventually drifted off to sleep.

The sun was high when we awoke. Without looking at my clock, I estimated it to be nearly mid-day given the sun's position - not quite nearly overhead like in midsummer, but well above the horizon. I could smell coffee and bacon, and it took me a few seconds to reorient myself to our situation and realize that Alex must be making late breakfast. Brighid was curled on her side, facing away from me, just starting to rouse herself. Pip had moved up to my pillow and was busy grooming himself. It was probably his fidgeting that woke me.

Brighid yawned and stretched. "Mmmm…bacon!"

I sat up and swung my legs over the side of the bed. Brighid got up and headed into the en suite. I set about gathering some clothes for us - we were close enough to the same size to share. She was taller though, which meant my skirts actually fell where they were meant to on her, instead of sweeping the floor like they do on me. Once we'd dressed, we strolled into the kitchen.

Alex was whistling as he flipped bacon in the pan. Where I usually cooked bacon in the oven, he seemed to prefer using a pan atop the stove. He'd already set out coffee cups for all of us. The table was set with plates and forks.

Brighid nudged me. "He's well domesticated," she whispered, with a wink.

"I think we can dispense with the potential boyfriend scenario now that you know the whole story," I hissed back. Still, I felt the heat rise to my cheeks.

"Mm? What was that?" Alex had turned to bring a plate of bacon to the table.

"Breakfast looks really great!" I said, a little too brightly. Brighid snorted.

"Coffee for everyone?" he asked. "Have a seat, ladies, it's nearly ready."

Brighid and I sat down. My stomach rumbled and I realized that we'd completely missed having any dinner last night. Alex and Lingus had been hunting the demon, and I'd been too nervous to eat anything anyway. Alex put on my oven mitt and reached into the oven to retrieve a warming plate stacked high with pancakes. He placed it on a trivet in the middle of the table and pivoted to get warmed syrup from the microwave. After pouring coffee and bringing it to the table, Alex sat down and we all started eating. I think it might have been the best breakfast I'd ever had.

With a familiar tingle in the base of my neck, I sensed the delivery truck about 30 seconds before I heard the rumbling of the engine and excused myself to go downstairs to meet them at the door. When I came back up, Alex and Brighid were arguing over who was going to do the tidying up.

"You cooked the breakfast, the least I can do is clean up!"

"Really, that isn't necessary."

I pushed the door shut with my butt. "Why don't you both wash up?"

They both turned to stare at me. After a couple of beats, Brighid shrugged and Alex nodded. I carried the box over to the coffee table as they set about cleaning the kitchen. Alex had already put the sofa back in order and I sat down and worked on opening the box. Whither hadn't let me down. Everything I'd asked for was in the box, and a couple of things I hadn't asked for, but that she obviously thought might be of use. That woman was a wonder.

I carefully placed everything out onto the coffee table. I sat and stared at it, hoping for inspiration.

Not having had any immediate flashes of inspiration, I suggested that the three of us pop down to the garden to see if Lingus and Adaine were there with any news. Adaine was nowhere to be seen, but Lingus was sitting near the fountain with the birds again. He stood and came toward us when we approached, and we convened on the patio, Lingus again sitting on the ground at the edge of the concrete.

"I hope you all rested well," Lingus said kindly.

"Yes thanks," I said. "We're eager to hear your news, if you have any."

He nodded. "We followed the demon. His lair is not far from here. He seems to have burrowed under the seabed about half a mile from the shoreline."

"Well, we can't take the trap to him. I can hold my breath, but I need to breathe to intone any spell associated with the trap." We were going to have to lure him out. I just wasn't sure where would be safest. The farther away from people, the better, of course.

"I was able to get close enough to him to lay a squall on him," Lingus said.

"A squall?" Alex leaned toward Lingus. "A sea storm? I don't understand."

"Not in that sense," Lingus said. "We refer to a...spell, for lack of a more appropriate comparison, that causes a disruption around something or someone a squall. I placed a squall on him intended to thwart his powers of attraction. To lessen his chances of preying upon other unsuspecting humans."

I shook my head. "Won't he notice something isn't right?"

Lingus shrugged. "Perhaps. But it is worth the effort to protect your kind. As he is still weakened, it may not be immediately obvious that his difficulty in luring prey is a result of an outside interference." I wasn't sure we wanted to know what would happen if he succeeded in luring someone into his clutches.

"Hey," Brighid said. "Where's your friend?"

"Adaine has remained near the lair. He will return to alert us when the demon becomes active."

I remembered my new protective ward then, and told them about it. "I can ward you as well, Lingus, if you'd like."

"Thank you, Morgaine, but that won't be necessary. We can not be harmed by demons."

"What?" How could they not be harmed? Demons were known to have a go at each other, what would stop them from having a go at Lingus or Adaine?

"As creatures of nature, we are incapable of being harmed by demons. Demons originated from ancient nature spirits. They can not directly cause permanent or debilitating harm to us, nor us to them."

That sent a bit of a shiver up my spine. Were demons and Daemons closely related enough to have common cause?

Alex seemed to have been having thoughts along the same lines. "But, you stand against them in this instance?"

"Oh, by all means we stand at cross purposes to them. But our ancient ties bind us from directly harming them."

"What about your squall?" I asked.

"It is causing the incubus no harm, merely disrupting his powers. He is free to return to his demesne, where the squall would have no effect."

I think I understood. "But, by aiding us, you do them indirect harm."

"Not harm, really." Lingus said, thoughtfully. "The demons have their purpose, and their demesne. This demon has breached its demesne, and we are in the right in assisting humans in restoring the balance."

That did make some sense. Eventually, Brighid and I left Alex and Lingus in the garden talking more about the origins of demons and Daemons, Alex having gone into to "scholar" mode. The first order of business was the protection ward.

Brighid squealed as the ward popped around her. "Oh, Mora, I'm impressed!"

"Thanks, sweetie! I promise to write it down for you to put in your own book of shadows when we get through this." We'd carried the treasures I'd been sent to the ritual space, and laid it all out within the circle. Now we settled in with my notes and Book of Shadows to try to work out how to fashion a trap for an incubus. I didn't know if anyone had ever attempted to trap a demon - not even a lesser one, let alone a major demon, even if it were being hosted by a human.

"So," Brighid said. "What about the other two witches who helped Alex previously? Any idea what they did?"

"No." I explained that he never wanted to know all the details of the traps. "I'm guessing we mightn't be allowed to publish our trap, either, although Alex hasn't specifically said that." I shuffled through some of the pages of notes I'd started. "At least, the lack of any reference to any sort of demon traps would suggest that."

"'Rules and restrictions'" we said in unison, without humor.

"Unless, of course, those were incidents that haven't taken place yet," she said. "Maybe YOUR trap will be basis of THEIRS!"

"An interesting idea, Brighid. But, I kind of doubt it. Otherwise, what would stop Alex or any of the other demon hunters having access to it? Their brains might then be a reference library for demons to get an idea of what to expect when confronted with a witch trying to trap them."

"Point."

I pushed the Book of Shadows over to her. Fresh eyes on the text may see something I missed. I carefully opened one of the books I'd pulled from my private collection, the first book of The Ænigmata, or "riddles", that had been passed down through my family. It was ancient and smelled of old libraries.

"What's that?" Brighid asked, waving her hand to dispel some dust that rose from the book when I'd opened it.

"It's a very old text. It contains accounts of hauntings, possessions, and spellwork that we wouldn't be able to find in any modern magical text." This was a dangerous volume as was the other book, the second volume of The Ænigmata and, to a lesser extent, the manuscript Whither had sent, for they contained accounts of dark magic and impious workings. Things that would prove very tempting to new, undisciplined witches, or those of questionable scruples. I was hesitant to let even Brighid consult these texts, and I trusted her implicitly.

After a time, I heard the scratching of Brighid's pencil on paper. It sounded like she was having some luck. I pulled my notebook closer and held my own pencil at the ready as I continued my perusal of the first volume of The Ænigmata. I flipped through the pages, scanning for anything that may give me some direction in creating the trap.

"Ugh. There is some disturbing stuff in this book. Descriptions of rituals I would never want to witness, let alone be involved in." I said. "Sick, sick stuff. No wonder witchcraft had got such a bad rap." It also explained why, though the volumes had been in our family for centuries, we never actually referenced them for workings. Instead they were just curiosities, collector's items.

Brighid smiled, looking up from her work. "I bet the workings in that book are about as far removed from the innocuous rituals and sabbats that got appropriated by other religions as you could get."

I nodded. "Yeah, you know the 'Malleus Maleficarum'?" She nodded. "Well, this text was written almost as a response to that. It incorporates the Christian concepts of demons, and is heavily inspired by the superstitions and fear of evil from those times. That's why there seems to be so much darkness in it."

"Hmm..." she twirled her pencil through her fingers thoughtfully. "Kind of like witchcraft through the veil of the worst of Christian hysteria."

"Exactly. It was written by a fringe faction of witches - yeah, we've had extremists in the broom closet before," I said to her raised eyebrows. "It isn't that those witches were evil, necessarily. But, given the times, and the persecution they were facing...well, desperate times... In any event, after the books were written, calmer heads prevailed and all copies of the Ænigmata were hidden away by a few trusted families. Mine was one of them. They were kept as a reminder of how dark things could get, and why meeting darkness with more darkness is not the best solution."

"Why even consult them?"

It was a fair question. "Well, I'm hoping I can find something that will help us, and if I do, I fully intend to modify it to distance our working from any dark magic associated with anything I find in the Ænigmata."

She nodded and we went back to our research. I was two-thirds of the way through the first book before I found anything promising. "I think I've found something…there is mention of a circle of symbols said to "hold fast" the subject of the working."

"That sounds pretty close to trapping."

I frowned. "Yeah, but the symbols were not recreated here, though. They're not even described." I made note of the page number for future reference and continued searching. I noted a few more pages before setting that book aside and searching the second volume. I had about the same amount of luck. Nothing definitive. There was, however, a chart of obscure rune symbols. I started another page of my notebook, reproducing symbols that might have some relevance in my trap. There were still very, very few references to traps, and they all seemed to refer to the same trap I'd originally found mentioned - that is, the arrangement of symbols to "hold fast" the subject. My last hope was the manuscript. It had no official title, but was known in magic circles as "The Scroll of Belphegor". I'd asked for it on a whim. Belphegor is said to be one of the seven princes of hell who wins souls by helping people make discoveries. And, well, I needed to make a discovery. I had no idea what the scroll contained, but it was worth a look, because I had no other ideas so far.

Before I could get very far into it, Alex came in. "Lingus gave me directions to where the demon's lair is. I'm going to go and look around."

"Let me ward you first," I said, gently pushing the books and papers aside and standing. I motioned him over and took both of his hands in mine. Closing my eyes, I began the intonation. As expected, I felt the electric zing of the spell forming, and then the "pop". I opened my eyes. Brighid was smiling. Alex looked alarmed. "What's wrong?"

"Nothing," he said. "That was amazing."

I blushed. "I have a really good book of shadows." I do admit to being proud of my protection ward, however. It had seemed to prove effective last night in shielding my true nature from the incubus.

"No, it's not just that," he said. "You have much power, Morgaine. This gives me great hope." He still held both of his hands in mine and now brought them up toward his face, turning them over, caressing my palms with his thumbs. A little shiver ran up each arm and I felt myself blushing again.

"Wow. No pressure, huh?" I was half-joking. In truth I was starting to despair of ever being able to fashion an appropriate trap for the demon.

He tilted his head to one side. "You can do this. WE can do this," he glanced at Brighid then, including her in the "we". She smiled. I know how badly she wanted to help. I was beginning to wonder if we would be able to keep her away when the working began.

When Alex left, Brighid and I resumed our searching. I smoothed the manuscript out and picked up where I'd left off. It was toward the end of the writing that I happened across the very thing I'd been searching for. Brighid noticed something was up - I must have been staring wide-eyed with my mouth hanging open - because she reached over and shook my shoulder.

"Whatcha got there, Mora?"

"Brighid, look at this!" I scooted over so we could both look at the scroll.

"That's possibly the closest thing to directions to making a magical trap we're ever likely to find!" she said. We read the section through twice, then I went back to the pages I'd noted in The Ænigmata.

"As best as I can tell," I said, "the working described in "The Scroll of Belphegor" is very similar to what was alluded to in The Ænigmata." I had a momentary dread that this had seemed too easy, and wondered if I'd have to give up my soul to one of the princes of Hell, but then it occurred to me that "too easy" would have been finding a fully formed working on my very first look. I'd been researching this for a couple of days now. Besides, witches don't believe in a "Hell" anyway. This spell wasn't exactly what I needed, but it was a solid groundwork on which to form the working we would need. As an added bonus, it didn't carry the same taint of dark magic as the Ænigmata, meaning it was a better choice to build upon. I could incorporate what I'd found in the Ænigmata without having to rely as heavily on those elements as the basis for the trap.

I looked up and smiled. "What we've got here, I believe, is the answer to our prayers."

"Um, we don't really pray, remember?"

I laughed. "No, but if we did..."

She smiled and pushed over her own notes. "Let's see what we can do then."

Chapter Seven

f we got through this, Brighid deserved as much credit as I did for fashioning this trap. She'd had some wonderful insights on incorporating certain parts of love spells to strengthen the working that would hopefully make luring the incubus easier. After spending an hour or so fashioning our disjointed scribblings into rough outline of a working, we grabbed our notes, the herbs and powders I'd been sent and some from the shop that we'd need and headed out to find Alex and the Daemons. Alex was in the living room on the sofa, a leather pouch opened in front of him on the coffee table. Several strange looking tools and small statuettes of mythological beings, often referred to as fetishes, were spread out across a leather wrapping in front of him. Most of the fetishes were of stone - some looking ancient, others looking brand new - but one was of wood. He was polishing an ornate athame with a soft cloth. Brighid and I sat on either side of him.

Brighid reached out toward the wooden fetish, a carved image of a horned being, its body twisted. "What are these?"

Alex gently grabbed her hand. "Ah, ah! Careful there. These are my tools for the banishing."

"But, I thought Mora said you weren't allowed magic?" Brighid asked.

"No, not as such. Nothing like what you ladies can do. Since the breach between planes, any further magical learning has been suspended for those who hunt the demons. I have been gifted with just this particular working, however. The power of the working has been imbued into me through ritual. But without these tools, I would not be able to do the banishment."

"Did you check out the lair?" I asked.

"Yes. It's about two-thirds of the way between here and where we found the demon last night. There is a build up of dunes there, not a lot of human habitation or traffic about." I think I knew the place he meant. "There was nothing there to suggest the presence of the demon. There is a bit of a sandbar about a half a mile out, visible at low-tide. I suspect that is where he's made his lair. Perhaps in an underwater cave beneath the sandbar."

It would be a well-hidden spot at high-tide, then.

Alex looked at me. "Have you had any luck?"

I smiled. "Quite a bit, actually. Brighid and I think we have created a perfect trap for the incubus." I indicated the items in my lap. "We were coming out to tell you and the Daemons about it."

Alex gathered up his own tools. "Let's go find them."

Adaine had returned and sat in quiet conversation with Lingus. It was nearly dusk already. We carried our things over to the patio and the three of us sat and spread our wares on the concrete near the edge where Lingus and Adaine sat.

"It appears you may have had some success," said Lingus, approvingly.

"I hope so," I said. "We are pretty confident."

"She nailed it," Brighid said, beaming. "I knew she could do it!"

"Not so fast, there - I couldn't have done it without you."

"It is good you have a plan," Adaine said, interrupting our mutual admiration society. "The demon is active earlier than expected. It is regaining strength."

"Where is it now?" I hoped we weren't out of time. I still wanted to tweak some of the working.

"It has returned to the pleasure dens where the humans gather. Luckily, Lingus' squall is still in place."

"I don't know how long it will last," Lingus said. "Adaine says the incubus has been traveling bar to bar in frustration seeking prey. It is feeding some off the usual emotional energies of the humans there, but that is not enough. In order to regain its full strength, it needs to find a human partner to feed upon. The stronger it grows, however, the less effect my squall will have."

I noticed Brighid shiver next to me. "I will probably regret asking this, but…what would have happened to me if… I mean…"

Lingus nodded, understanding. "Sexual energy is one of the strongest powers in existence. It is why a number of your rituals and spells utilize sex, to strengthen the intent of your workings. Incubi and succubi are traditionally dream demons, so their effect on humans is essentially harmless in that humans can quickly regain emotional or psychic strength lost when they are visited by one of the demons in a dream. This incubus is now made flesh, and the damage to humans will be exponentially greater, and would likely include physical damage as well. As it has never happened before, we can not know for certain, but I suspect a human that falls prey to this demon could very well be irreparably damaged, emotionally as well as physically. In order to sustain its current form, I fear what would be taken from the human during the seduction and subsequent coupling would be irreplaceable. I don't know if they could survive, and could possibly perish either as a result of the physical damage of the coupling, or by their own hand as a result of the emotional damage."

I took Brighid's hand and squeezed it tightly. This incubus was really starting to piss me off.

I indicated the things we'd spread out on the patio. "These are part of what we can use for our trap. I showed Lingus the diagram I'd made of the proposed circle I hoped to trap the incubus in. Alex averted his gaze, keeping to his less-known-the-better plan, and I kept my words regarding the plan to a minimum. "With this, and the herbs and powders we have, I think it will be strong enough to hold the demon."

"Once Morgaine has trapped it," Alex rolled the leather cloth open to reveal his tools, "I am ready to banish it."

I stood then and the others followed. I lead them out into the open part of the garden, the space reserved for the store's public ceremonies and rituals. "This space should be large enough to form the circle. Since there are very few residences nearby, and we are likely to be performing our working after the few businesses that remain open year-round have closed for the day, I think we can safely set up the trap here. Then, we just have to lure the incubus to it."

Suddenly, the hair on the back of my neck stood on end. Something wasn't right. I looked over at Brighid. I could tell she was sensing something too. "Did you feel that?"

"What is it?" Alex asked.

"I don't know." I looked over to where Lingus and Adaine stood to see that they, too, were on guard. At that moment a fireball landed and burst at my feet, catching my skirt alight. Alex hastily patted the flame out before it could spread and we all looked up. A strange creature was perched in the tree in the corner, cackling. It was squat, grey-skinned, and hairless, with large reddish eyes and an over-sized nose and ears. I could see its hand raised, forming another fireball. Another sound caught my attention and I turned. A second such creature was hovering in the air above the garden, forming its own fireball. The first one loosed its weapon then, the fireball bursting at Lingus' feet this time.

"Imps!" he said, turning toward the creature and holding his hands aloft, silently intoning some magic of his own. More fireballs hit the ground around us then and I looked around to see a swarm of the imps materializing above us.

"Run!" I shouted, and Alex, Brighid and I turned toward the shop. Imps began swooping in front of us, trying to block our escape. Lingus directed some sort of energy in our direction that seemed to repel the imps.

"Get to your home," he said. "Adaine and I will try to dismiss these creatures."

We started moving, the imps harrying us by swooping as close as Lingus' energy bubble would allow. Fireballs continued dropping and bursting. Patches of grass began to smolder. I worried that if the imps didn't take us out with the fireballs, they'd wind up causing a fire that would. We made our way, zig-zagging to avoid the swooping imps, to the side of the shop and rushed inside. We ran up the stairs to the ritual room and looked out of the window to observe the fight outside. Pip was on the window sill, hissing and growling. There were dozens of imps now, Lingus and Adaine doing all they could to keep them at bay. The late-season remains of flowerbeds smoldered and several of my bushes were ablaze. I couldn't understand how they were doing it - I had numerous protective wards on my property. The wards on the shop and flat were even stronger, and I could only hope the imps would not be able to breach them. Brighid began intoning a spell, and the fires began diminishing. Almost as soon as she could put one out, however, another fireball hit the ground and lit grass and branches anew. I quickly grabbed my Book of Shadows, flipped to the strongest banishing spell I could find and started casting it.

It seemed the siege might never end, Lingus and Adaine using their powers, Brighid concentrating on putting out the fires, and me intoning the banishment over and over, but eventually it grew quiet. The attack was over. Brighid and I were ready to collapse from the exertion. Pip was pacing beneath the window now, hackles lowered, but still uttering low growls.

"Gods, I'm glad that's over," I said, peering down at my scorched lawn.

"For someone who's always getting onto me about not wearing my protective charms, I would have thought you'd have at least a basic protection ward on your property."

I spun to glare at Brighid. Her nerves were not the only ones raw. "I DO have protections on this property! I would have had to release them when we lured the incubus into the trap, but I haven't done that yet. I have no idea how those imps breached them. I'm just thankful the wards on the building held."

"Oh, hey, I'm so sorry," she said, coming over to hug me. "I'm sorry I snarled at you. It's just…that was intense."

I hugged her back. "I know. It's OK. Will you help me renew the wards?"

"Yeah, of course."

"We'd better go check on Lingus and Adaine." I looked over Brighid's shoulder and saw Alex in the reading chair, his head in his hands.

I walked over and knelt in front of him, sliding my hands onto his knees. "Hey…you OK?"

He looked up and met my eyes. He looked as exhausted as I felt. "I was useless." He raked his hands through his hair and broke eye contact. "You and Brighid were slinging spells, Lingus and Adaine were doing their nature guardian thing. Even Pip was yowling down all the hosts of heaven, and I wasn't doing anything."

I smiled and reached for one of his hands. "Don't beat yourself up. You said yourself you aren't allowed to access magic, except for your banishing work."

"I should have been able to do something!"

"Don't." I said. "This was nothing compared with what's to come. We will need you on top form for the banishment."

He nodded, still seeming a little defeated though.

Brighid took a step toward us. "We could teach you…"

He favored her with a small smile. "Thank you, I'd really like that, but I'm afraid it would mean giving up my role as a demon hunter. I could be a witch, or a demon hunter, but not both."

"Rules and restrictions?" she asked.

He nodded. "Yes. But, damn it, next time I want to be out there swinging a cricket bat, or *something*, at least!"

"Come on," I said. "Let's go see how the Daemons are."

Lingus and Adaine were both lying on the lawn, not moving. I ran over to them calling their names. Lingus stirred and sat up, followed soon after by Adaine. I heaved a sigh of relief. "Are you two OK?"

"Yes, thank you, just drained."

I collapsed on the lawn next to him. "I don't know how that happened. I have wards all over this place."

Lingus shook his head. "It would appear that we may have been discovered. Perhaps the incubus has regained sufficient strength to enable those imps to breach your defenses. Were you attacked inside?"

"No, thankfully. Those wards held."

"Morgaine," Lingus looked me in the eye. "You should understand that those imps could easily have destroyed you. They were endowed with a strength they would not normally possess, and were quite capable of hitting you directly with their fire. I believe this attack was merely intended to rattle you, perhaps to the point that you would abandon your duty." That would seem to mean that the demon was on to us, but I couldn't see how that could be. He certainly couldn't have suspected I was a witch from the brief contact we'd had, and he hadn't followed us that night, so he shouldn't know where I lived, regardless.

"Guys..." Brighid was standing near the patio. She looked up from the ground to me and shook her head. I walked over to her, followed by Alex. Lingus and Adaine struggled to their feet to join us. On the patio where we'd laid out our tools were piles of ash. The powders and herbs I'd got from Whither, and anything flammable of Alex's banishment tools. I looked up at Alex. His face was stricken. Lingus stooped and sifted the ash a bit. The metal and stone parts of Alex's kit remained, but the handles for some of the tools and the twisted wooden fetish were gone, destroyed by the imps' fireballs.

He looked at me. "We are lost."

I shook my head. "We're not out yet. I can get more of the herbs and powders. I can remake my notes. The stone remains, and we can fashion new handles for the iron."

He shook his head slowly, sadly. "The wooden fetish was integral to the banishment, and it is gone."

We stood, looking from one to the other. No one spoke. There was nothing left to say in that moment. I knew we couldn't just give up, though. Too much depended on our success. I looked to the sky. It was a clear night, a blanket of stars above. I could even make out the Milky Way. There had to be another way…something we could do to set things to rights. As important as the tools were, surely our intent was just as essential and a strong part, if not the strongest part, of the working. I slid my hand into Alex's and squeezed. He joined me in looking at the stars. Eventually, I felt Brighid's hand slide into my free one. I glanced down. Lingus and Adaine had moved to join us, taking hands with Alex and Brighid. The five of us stood in an impromptu circle around our ruined tools, surrounded by my still smoldering garden. I looked back up at the sky and sent a silent but fervent petition to any benevolent beings paying attention. *"Help us. Please."*

We were all exhausted. Brighid and I worked to enforce the wards around the property, Lingus and Adaine adding strength to them with some of their own powers. Alex salvaged as many of his tools from the ashes as he could. It seemed the only irreparable damage was the loss of the wooden fetish. I kept hoping there might be a way around it.

Even Brighid was grasping for any possible workaround. "Can't you just go back in time and warn yourself, or, I don't know, bring the fetish back from the past?"

Alex's expression was thunderous, but he met my eye and I saw the frustration give a little. "That would seem the obvious thing to do," he was astoundingly gentle in his response, a true gentleman despite the fact he may have wanted to yell instead, "but the laws of physics do not allow for the paradoxes that would be caused, and the rules and restrictions in place for us would prevent it even if we could somehow circumvent physics."

Lingus and Adaine had retired to their place in my garden. I wasn't sure exactly where within the garden they were staying. They sort of vanished. If they used some sort of misdirection so that we didn't see where they went, I couldn't say, but none of us humans could tell what had happened to them after we'd said our "good nights".

I made the call to arrange for another shipment of some of the supplies that were destroyed. Having laid out the beginnings of a plan for trapping the incubus, I had a better idea of which items I'd need, and it turned out that a good deal of what I'd need was readily available in my own collection. Our main problem was the loss of the wooden fetish. Alex was adamant that it was an imperative part of the banishment.

"Is there any chance there is another like it somewhere?" I asked as the three of us sat picking at our takeaway meals later in the living room.

"Not that I'm aware of." He pushed his teriyaki chicken around in its container. "I can return to our base. It is all I can think of to do now."

Brighid said, "But if there is more than one of you doing this, there has to be more of the fetishes, right? Couldn't you borrow one from a teammate or something?"

"Oh, my dear Brighid, if only it were that simple. Each fetish is bonded to its holder. And, there aren't that many of us anyway."

"Your amulet," I began. "Does it…speak to you?" I'd remembered the sense I'd had of something sentient probing my mind when I'd touched it that day at the cafe. Brighid looked from one to the other of us, intrigued. We'd explained that Alex possessed an amulet that allowed him to travel in time, but this was the first she'd heard of the amulet's sentience. Before she had a chance to launch an interrogation, I held up my hand. "I promise I'll explain later".

"Not so much in the way you would expect. It sends impressions, I guess is the best way to explain it. It has given me the impression that I should return to our base for advice."

I nodded. "When will you go?"

"Soon. Perhaps while you and Brighid rest. I should be back by the time you wake." I picked up on an undercurrent of insecurity in his voice. I guessed that there might be a possibility that he wouldn't be back. I wondered if any traveler had lost a fetish before, and what the consequences might be. I didn't fear that he would be punished, really. But, there was the possibility that another demon hunter would have to be sent in his place. That saddened me. I felt that a bond was forming between us, a trust that might not come naturally with anyone else. I feared the working would not be as strong without Alex's presence. I feared I wouldn't be as strong without him near.

We sat in silence a while, picking at our food. Each of us forcing bites down without any real notice of the flavors. Swallowing nutrition, not enjoying the food.

"If the demon is on to us," I said, "it will be seeking to regain its strength even more quickly now. The longer we delay, the stronger the demon could become." While I was confident in my trapping spell, executing it with the demon at full or near-full strength would be very difficult. It would almost assuredly employ more imps and other lesser demons to harass us as we worked. Lingus and Adaine were, so far, the only two nature Daemons who had stepped forward to help. Lingus had already relayed the danger to other Daemons and only Adaine had attended. I didn't know if asking Lingus to appeal to them again would help. What if it just annoyed them and solidified their resistance to come to our aid? The Fae were a fickle lot.

"I can't see how the demon could have worked it out about us so soon," Alex said. "Unless he's already stronger than he seems." That was a sobering prospect.

When we could no longer force any more food down, we decided to call it a night. Lingus had said he felt we should be safe the rest of the night. That this attack had been more of a warning shot than anything. He was confident in the strength of the new wards, and promised he and Adaine would remain vigilant through the night. Brighid went off to shower and get ready for bed. I stayed to sit with Alex a while.

After several minutes of sitting silently staring straight ahead, I felt his hand enclose mine. "I don't know what will happen when I get back to base," he said.

"I know." He'd obviously been thinking about the chance he would not be allowed to return as well.

"Whatever happens, I want you to know that I have the utmost faith in you, Morgaine. I believe your spell will work. I have no doubt that it is solid magic, and you've imparted your own strengths to it."

"Alex, don't talk like you're not coming back."

He turned to look at me then. "It may be necessary to send another hunter. We have to accept that fact. Even if there is a way for me to regain the fetish, or acquire a new one, there may not be enough time before it's too late."

I shook my head. "But you are a time-traveler. How can there not be enough time? Can't you just go back, get another fetish - even if it takes years - and just return to us in time?" It seemed perfectly reasonable to me.

"Rules and restrictions," he said, simply. Those two words were quickly becoming my least favorite of the vocabulary. "Once an event is in motion, there are unbendable limitations on how much leeway we have in taking advantage of our ability to manipulate time." He squeezed my hand. "I am sorry." Damn those rules and restrictions. I could understand their necessity in some instances, but in a case like this, they just seemed more harmful than helpful.

I looked him in the eyes. Such beautiful eyes. I really didn't know if I could do this without him.

As if he'd read my mind, he gave me a small smile and leaned in toward me. A strand of hair had come loose from his make-shift ponytail and fell across his cheek. "You CAN do this." I had the sense that he might just lean further forward and kiss me, then. I wasn't sure that I didn't want him to do just that.

Pip, on the other hand, seemed to have other plans. He took that very moment to leap onto the sofa between us. He put his paws on Alex's chest and head butted him on the chin. The darn cat seemed to realize Alex was about to leave, and wanted to make sure to get in his goodbye. Alex dropped my hand and cuddled Pip for a bit. Then he stood.

"No sense in putting it off," he said. "Might as well go now and see what can be done." I nodded, not trusting myself to words just then. He smiled, laid his hand across his heart and bowed slightly. Then, he closed his eyes and was gone.

I sat for several minutes, numb. I decided to take it as a good sign that another demon hunter hadn't appeared immediately. Eventually, I made my way to the bedroom. Brighid was already asleep, the covers clutched tightly around her. I pushed a bit of hair back from her face and bent down to kiss her forehead before heading into the en suite to shower. I stood and let the hot water flow over me for a while, easing some of the stress from my muscles. I chose my calming shower gel as well. The best thing I could do right now was to attempt to get as much rest as possible. Whatever happened next, if Alex would return or not, there was nothing I could do about it in that moment. Even still, I sent up a humble invocation to my spirit guides to lend their aid in bringing him back to me.

Once I'd got into bed and turned off the lamp, the exhaustion overtook me, and I was asleep almost immediately. I would have expected either a dreamless sleep, or one filled with nightmares after the trauma of the previous hours, but instead, I found myself dreaming of a sunny apple grove. The sweet, heady smell of ripe apples filled the air as I walked, barefooted, beneath the bows of the trees which stretched over the path to form a verdant, sun-dappled cathedral. I was dressed in a simple shift of undyed lawn, my hair loose around my shoulders. A back-lit figure stood on the path, several trees ahead of me. As I drew closer, the indistinct figure resolved into that of a woman. She was small, not quite as tall as me, even - maybe 5'2". Her skin was a swarthy, earthy tone like a milky cup of tea or the color of desert sand shaded by a dune, her eyes a deep, sparkling green. Long dark hair fell in loose waves to her waist. Her shift was dyed blue, simple and plain. A length of rope was knotted around her waist, a hand-held scythe and a bundle of herbs bound with twine tied to it. A silver circlet with Celtic knotwork sat upon her forehead, a small woad crescent tattooed between her brows. Her coloring and features were just different enough to mark her as not entirely human. She stood with her arms to her sides, slightly raised with palms out, an inviting stance. I could not help but smile as I approached, serenity emanating from her in warm waves to encircle me. Overcome with peace and awe, I fell to my knees before her and bowed my head. This was a queen. A queen of the Fae. This was Morgaine.

She took my face gently in her hands and lifted my gaze to hers. "My namesake. My child. Rise, and walk with me."

I did as she bid and we continued along the tree lined path that seemed to have no end. "You have been called to a difficult task," she said. "You do not walk alone. Know that my grace is upon you."

"Thank you, Lady," I said.

She linked her arm in mine. My skin tingled where it touched hers. "He will come back to you."

I could only imagine she meant Alex. Did this mean he found another fetish, or some other method to complete his work?

"He will need your assistance to restore what was lost. You will need to give much of your magic to this. What is given may weaken your own working later, but the demon must not be allowed to remain within the human plane."

I dare not ask her to be any clearer. If this was, as I suspected, a prophetic dream, it was best to keep quiet and absorb as much information as possible, and try to figure it all out later.

"Now," she said. She stopped walking and turned to face me, taking both my hands in hers. She stood tall, reaching to kiss me on my forehead, then each of my eyelids, and then my lips. "It is time for you to return. He comes."

But, this couldn't be the end of the dream - it was too soon to go. I needed more information. What could I do to help Alex? What would be required of me? What did it mean that I would have to give much of my magic? Would my magic be forever weakened? Before I had a chance to say anything, the dream began to fade. Morgaine reached up and began gently shaking my shoulder. The shaking continued as the dream evaporated, and as I opened my eyes, I found that it was Alex shaking me gently awake. "Hi," he said quietly.

I sat up and enclosed him into a hug with such force I nearly pulled him over onto the bed. Even though Morgaine had told me he would return, I very nearly couldn't believe it. "You came back."

I released him and glanced over at Brighid. She was still fast asleep. I looked back at Alex. He motioned for me to follow. I slipped out of the bed, followed by Pip who'd been dozing on my pillow. Looking at the bedside clock, I saw the time was a quarter to four. I'd been asleep less than two hours. I followed Alex out into the hallway and gently closed the bedroom door. The dream was still fresh in my mind. The strength of it such that the scent of apples seemed to permeate my flat. I ached for the presence of Morgaine but a sense of abiding peace remained from the dream, as well.

We walked down the hallway to the ritual room. A piece of driftwood about a foot long and around 5" in diameter was on the floor within the circle. Next to it was a paper towel with what looked like ashes from the remains of our items that got damaged or destroyed on the patio. Alex picked up the driftwood. "The good news is that there is a way forward. Because of the nature of the fetishes, how they came into our possession, and the way they are attuned to each of us, there is no replacement. That's part of why there aren't very many of us demon hunters - there were only so many of the fetishes, you see. Since that particular fetish was bonded to me, I will need to recreate it as closely as possible within a ritual that should bind the power I shared with the original fetish to the newly created one. I spent about an hour and a half searching along the beach near where the demon has made its lair to find this driftwood. When I found this piece and came back here, I collected some of the ashes from our things." He gestured to the pile of ashes. "I can use the athame blade for carving." He hesitated.

"What's the bad news, then?"

"Well, not so much *bad* news. But, there is some difficulty involved." He reached into his pocket and handed me a piece of paper. "I will need to do the carving within a ritual, in order to bond me to the fetish, and to bond the spell of banishment within it. This is a list of requirements for the ritual. Candles, herbs, powders…" he paused, "and a basic overview of what the ritual will entail."

I scanned the list. Luckily, all of the requirements could be found in either the shop, or my personal collection. The ritual itself, however, was completely new to me. It would be a long ritual - hours, if not a full day or more - and it would require my complete concentration. The words of the ritual were unknown to me, but at various stages of the ritual, I would be required to chant them without hesitation. This ritual would take my complete and unrestrained confidence. It would also require freely giving of my spirit as well as of my body. I wondered if Alex was aware of what that would mean. The power binding part of the ritual would involve the two of us becoming one. In the carnal sense. Male and female witches performed such rites when required, regardless of their personal relationship outside of the circle. Alex was not a witch. And, in our case, it would mean having sex without the preamble of a fully formed emotional relationship - either as romantic partners, or magical working partners. I read over it again before I looked up at him. "Do you understand all that is required, of both of us, in this ritual?"

He nodded. "Yes. Are you willing?"

I didn't need to think about it. I felt a tingle of anticipation, actually. But, regardless of how comfortable I felt with Alex, what needed to be done was too important to even consider saying no. "I am. Have you ever been involved in such a ritual before?"

"No. The original binding of the fetish to me was quite different," he said, thoughtful. "I can only assume others performed...the other part of the ceremony."

I nodded. "Yes, that part involves binding the power within the fetish." A separate ritual would have been performed, by two skilled witches, to imbue the fetish with its power. Binding the fetish to Alex would have been a simpler ritual performed at a later date. This was essentially the two rituals combined. I understood now what Morgaine had meant when she said I would need to give much of my magic to this. I would be performing a double ritual, including one that called upon the magic of two witches. I would also be pouring my magic into the carving as it was created. While Alex would physically participate and would serve as a conduit of the magic, the working's actual magic would be drawn from and by me alone. It would weaken me considerably. I could only hope I would be able to recover enough to carry through with the trapping of the demon when the time came.

Alex took a step toward me. "I wouldn't ask this of you lightly."

I grabbed his hand and squeezed it. "I know. Morgaine came to me in a dream just before you returned. She alerted me that something was required that would use much of my magic. But with her grace, I can do this. If you are at all uneasy, there are things we can do to make it easier. There are spells I can cast to help with relaxation, lowering inhibitions…"

He smiled and squeezed my hand back. "No. I enter into this with the full knowledge of what we must do. What is it you say in beginning a circle? In perfect love and perfect trust? Morgaine, I have come to trust in you completely, despite our relatively short acquaintance. I don't think I could do this - I wouldn't want to do this - with anyone else." Was it wishful thinking on my part to imagine that the intensity in his gaze suggested his feelings might involve even more than trust? We had only known each other a handful of days, but it felt as if we'd known each other longer, so strong was my trust in him, and my desire to be near him.

"But, what if…" he hesitated. "I mean, I presume we must do this ritual without…anything between us. That is, no protection against pregnancy."

"Oh, that," I bit back a laugh. "No, there's no chance. I have methods both mundane and magical to guard against that. And, also wards that will protect against any transmission of diseases," I winced a bit at saying that. I hoped he wouldn't think I was alluding to any past indiscretions of his as putting his or my health in danger, but these sorts of precautions must be considered.

"Ah, well, I can assure you that I am free of anything of that nature - my health was tested extensively upon becoming a member of…my group. But, I am glad you are attentive to such matters."

"I didn't mean to imply that you weren't in top health, I just wanted to reassure you that there are ways of being safe —"

"No, of course - I didn't think you meant anything like that," he smiled. "I am most pleased that you look out for yourself in all things, though."

I smiled and nodded, relieved. "Now then, you should go shower - try not to wake Brighid. Eat something if you are hungry. I'll begin the preparations." He nodded and left me alone in the ritual room with just Pip and my own thoughts. I had been given a great honor, and a great responsibility. This binding of power to the fetish was a very advanced magic, and was likely only ever performed by highly ascended witches long associated with Alex's time-travel society. Perhaps even by Morgaine herself in the company of another strong witch. This combined ritual was unique in that it called for binding Alex to the fetish before binding the power within it. I speculated that this might serve to make the magic even stronger, and Alex's banishing work even more powerful.

I grabbed my besom and began the ritual cleansing of the space. Pip took his place in the reading chair. As I swept the space, I made it into a meditation, clearing my mind and invoking my spirit guides to ask for protection and guidance in the work to come. Once I'd cleansed the space, I went down to the shop to collect the things we would need. Back in the flat, I started preparing the circle in the ritual room, and then composed a letter to Brighid, letting her know what was happening so she wouldn't walk in on us unawares. She would understand that we would require as much quiet as possible and that we could not be disturbed before the ritual was complete. I asked if she would be our guard, and do her best to work with Lingus and Adaine to protect us should we come under attack again. Since it would soon be morning, I hoped we would be safe from imps and other lesser demons, but we couldn't be too confident that they wouldn't mount another attack, especially if they sensed the magical working. I called Lingus up to the window of the ritual room and told him what was about to happen.

"I wish you the best, Morgaine. It is a difficult undertaking."

I nodded. "It could be hours - it may even last all day and into the next night. Just the carving alone will be time-consuming, and then the rest…" I trailed off.

"We will do everything in our power to keep you and Alex safe." He bowed and floated back downward, disappearing into my garden. I lowered the window, leaving just enough of an opening for fresh air. Alex came back to the ritual room fresh from the shower with only a towel around his waist. Having had a shower just before bed, I was as ready as I was ever going to be. Although seeing him there in just a towel…suddenly I was nervous. There was nothing for it but to push that feeling aside and concentrate on the importance of what we had to do. I crossed the room and closed the door.

Chapter Eight

Knowing that we would be kneeling for a long period of time, I had retrieved several padded mats from my closet to reduce the pressure on our knees. We would need to remain as comfortable as possible so that aches and pains did not distract us from the ritual. I had arranged all of the tools I'd need on the floor near the center of the circle. Alex's driftwood, ash, and athame blade were ready for him. A small brazier was ready to be lit. I'd placed several extra disks of charcoal nearby, as I didn't want to risk running out. My herbs and powders were arranged in the quantities and order in which I would need them. I had placed the elemental candles and offering bowls in the four quarters. I retrieved my athame from the wall, as well as my salt dispenser. I wanted that extra layer of protection for this working.

I faced Alex. "Ready?"

"As I'll ever be," he smiled.

We walked into the circle. My back to Alex, I shimmied out of my nightgown and tossed it outside of the circle. Moments later, I heard the thump of Alex's towel. Taking a deep breath, I faced him again. He was a truly beautiful man. He returned my appreciative gaze, and I felt the heat in my cheeks as the blood rose. I could already feel the magical energy rising within the circle. There was a tingling in my core and as my eyes traveled over Alex's body, from his broad shoulders downward, I had the distinct impression that he felt it too. I stepped around him and walked the perimeter of the scorched circle, laying down the salt circle, leaving a small opening.

I retrieved the box of long matches from the floor and struck one, handing it to Alex. We began in the east of the circle, lighting the candle of the eastern guard:

"Guardians of the East, I call upon thee to watch over the rites of this casting. Powers of knowledge and wisdom, guided by Air, we ask thee to keep watch over us, tonight within this circle."

We moved to the south and I felt Alex move in closer to me.

"Guardians of the South, I call upon thee to watch over the rites of this casting. Powers of passion and will, guided by Fire, we ask thee to keep watch over us, tonight within this circle."

Moving to the west, Alex laid his free hand lightly on my hip as he bent to light the candle.

"Guardians of the West, I call upon thee to watch over the rites of this casting. Powers of empathy and emotion, guided by Water, we ask thee to keep watch over us, tonight within this circle."

We walked together to the north. As he bent to light the candle, Alex's hair, now unconstrained by the ribbon he usually wore, brushed across my breast, sending a frisson of excitement through my body.

"Guardians of the North, I call upon thee to watch over the rites of this casting. Powers of endurance and strength, guided by Earth, we ask thee to keep watch over us, tonight within this circle." Traveling to the center of the circle, I took the match from Alex and lit the brazier.

I placed the matches outside of the circle and picked up the salt dispenser again. "Enter we now into this consecrated circle, in perfect love and in perfect trust," I said, closing the circle. I motioned for Alex to take his place and went to my own. I placed a disk of charcoal into the cast iron grate of the brazier and allowed it to heat. Then as he set to begin the carving, I intoned a blessing on Alex and his work, placing mugwort and angelica on the charcoal. I pricked my finger with my boline, a small ritual knife, and allowed three small drops of blood to fall onto the herbs, a symbol of my intent to sacrifice of myself for the success of this working.

As Alex carved, I intoned portions of the spell, tossed herbs or powders on the charcoal at the appropriate intervals, and concentrated on pulling power into the circle. It got noticeably warmer as we worked and before long, both of our bodies bore a sheen of perspiration regardless of the cool air circulating from the window. As I intoned the strange words, I hoped I was doing the pronunciation justice. My grandmother had taught me that in situations like these, the best you could do is intone the words with as much confidence as possible and trust the Lord and Lady to divine your meaning.

An hour passed, maybe more. Alex concentrated on the carving. He had hacked the wood down to a smaller size quickly when we began, but now had slowed his work to coax the details of the figure out as closely to the original as possible. The fetish was starting to take shape, the curve of the body emerging from the wood. All the while, I intoned the words of the spell intended to bind the fetish to him, replacing the charcoal when needed and using more of the herbs and powders for the working. At this point both of us were in a near trance-like state, aware of nothing but each other and the work.

I don't know for sure how much more time passed before Alex finally put his athame down, rubbed the new carving with consecrated oil and then with the ashes left from the attack, and looked up at me. He was finished. He'd done a remarkable job. As far as I could tell he'd fashioned a perfect replica of the lost fetish. It was time to complete the second part of the ritual.

He stood and crossed to where I knelt, and dropped to his knees beside me. I cast the powders to mark the beginning of the power infusing ritual on the charcoal, and intoned the opening words.

Alex and I turned to face each other. I smiled at him. "Ready?"

He glanced downward and I followed his gaze. He was indeed ready. He looked back up, smiling. He laid his hand on my cheek, drawing his thumb gently across my lips. His full erection and his eyes told me all I needed to know, but still he said "Yes."

Between the aromas of the magical herbs and powders, and the strength of the magic surrounding us in our circle, my desire for him had risen. The concentration of the previous part of the spell, as well as the power of the magical working, meant any nervousness we might have had about what was to come was gone. We were ready. As I was the source and conduit of the magic of the ritual, I assumed the dominant position, gently pushing Alex back onto the mat. I placed the paper with the words of the spell next to his head.

"Be gentle with me," he teased.

"Shush," I said, smiling despite my attempt to sound stern.

I took the fetish from him and placing it between my thighs against my sex, said the words of power invoking the necessary magic into the carved wooden figure. There was a quick intake of breath from Alex as, moving the fetish to hold it against his member, I repeated the words. Feeling the wetness of my desire flood my sex, I straddled Alex and slowly lowered myself onto him. A jolt of energy flowed through my core as he entered me, filling me fully. I placed the fetish between my breasts and lay forward so that it was wedged between us at the heart chakra. It was my turn to gasp then.

"Are you OK?" Alex asked, creasing his brow in concern.

I nodded. "Yeah - it's your amulet." When I lay forward my breast, just above my heart, came to rest with the amulet between us. Though it was normally "embedded" in his chest, when our skin touched over the raised impression of the amulet, it materialized as it had that day at the cafe when he first showed it to me. "Just got a bit of a tingle from it is all."

Alex smiled and nodded. It wasn't just a tingle, however. Again, I felt the touch of another sentience in my mind, as if the intelligence within the amulet was exploring my thoughts. At first it was disconcerting, which is what caused me to gasp, but soon it felt soothing. It was as if the amulet were providing an even deeper connection between me and Alex. Perhaps adding it's own inscrutable magic to the work.

Slowly, locking eyes with Alex, I began moving, releasing him and drawing him back into me again and again. His lips parted and he gave a soft sigh as I increased my pace. His eyes were half closed, but still locked on mine. I could see the pleasure building within him as I continued to move. He placed his hands on my hips, gently adjusting my pace. We moved together, urgently for a span, then slowing, then increasing the pace again as our pleasure built closer to a climax. I nearly lost myself in his eyes, having to force my mind back to the ritual, to concentrate on drawing the power through us and into the fetish. The feel of him inside me, of his hands on my body, was intoxicating.

He lifted a hand to caress my cheek. "You are beautiful," he breathed. "Glowing…it's…I've never…" I gently laid a finger over his lips. As wonderful as his words were, as thrilling as the feel of him moving inside me was, I had to try to concentrate.

We increased our pace again, the pleasure building, almost spilling over. I focused on his eyes, willing my mind to draw the power through us, concentrating on matching his passion. Alex grabbed my hand, entwining our fingers, his other hand on the small of my back. With one final thrust, I felt him release inside of me, a low moan escaping his parted lips. I let myself go then, matching his orgasm with my own, concentrating on releasing the built up power into the fetish. I barely managed to whisper the final words of the ritual, binding the power within the fetish. Exhausted, I lay on top of him with my head resting against his shoulder, both of our hearts rapidly beating in time, our breathing labored with the exertion. The fetish felt hot between us, almost scalding against our skin. Waves of pleasure continued to spread through me, punctuated by the gentle throbbing of his member. I don't know how long we lay like that, limbs entwined, our bodies still connected at the core. Eventually, Alex rolled us onto our sides, remaining inside of me. He moved the fetish, still warm but cooling, from between us and held me tightly. As the amulet fell away from me, I felt the sentience withdraw. I felt at peace.

I think we may have dozed for a short time. When I opened my eyes again, he was no longer inside me, but his arms were still around me. I moved to prop myself up on my elbow. He rolled onto his back and looked up at me.

"I'm not entirely sure, not being an expert at this sort of thing, but I think we might have achieved a measure of success," he smiled.

"I'm pretty sure we did. And I think the fetish is fully charged, too." We both laughed then, relief mixed with the afterglow. "I think we can finish now." I pushed myself up to a sitting position, surprised at the effort it took. Alex stood and offered his hand to help me up. I really was exhausted. I didn't let go of him as I stood. Raising my athame, I saluted the guardians of the four quarters and thanked them for their guidance and protection. I let go of Alex's hand. He went around the circle, putting out the candles as I bid farewell to the guardians one by one. Then Alex and I walked, hand in hand, to the edge of the circle. The last coal in the brazier had burned out at some point after the end of the ritual. I made the circle-opening cutting motions to the right and the left - creating a "door" in our circle. I pushed aside the salt with a swish of my foot and we left the circle. I glanced at the window. It was dark outside. I couldn't believe we'd finished before daybreak. More likely than not, an entire day had passed while we were within the circle.

Alex had collected his athame blade and placed it and the fetish on one of my shelves as we passed. Clean up could wait. We didn't even bother with covering ourselves, we just opened the door and walked down the hallway toward my bedroom and straight into the en suite shower. We took turns washing each other, extending the ritual a little while longer, still thrumming from the pleasure we'd taken of each other. Stepping out of the shower, we dried each other off before stumbling into bed and falling deeply asleep. Brighid would have to sleep on the sofa-bed tonight.

 had no dreams that night. I woke up aching all over. It had been an intense ritual. We'd finished and gone to bed before I could really process everything that had happened. Namely, my near loss of concentration when we… when we… I wasn't even sure what to call it. There is always some emotional involvement between the Priestess and Priest (or however they've designated themselves) during a sex magic ritual - that's part of the power of the working - but, usually it's emotions born of mutual respect and a genuine friendship. Of course there are participants who conduct the rite with their real-world lovers or spouses. Those rites can be even more powerful given the love the two share, although if things are a bit dicey for them outside of the ritual circle, that can impact the power of the working as well. When Alex and I performed that part of the ritual, I experienced some intense desire for him. Part of that can certainly be attributed to the ritual itself, and the heightened senses the working can inspire. But I'd been so distracted by the desire that I'd very nearly missed part of the wording. I'd caught myself, yes, but

it still alarmed me just how impassioned I'd been. For his part, Alex seemed fairly impassioned as well, but then, that was pretty much his part in it anyway. He hadn't been required to conduct any of the ritual - what to say and when to say it, what herbs or powders were required and when - he didn't need to concentrate on drawing power into the fetish. Even with a cheat sheet, it was challenging. All he was required to do was attain an orgasm. No, that wasn't entirely fair. He, too, had to keep the goal of the working in mind, even if he didn't need to concentrate on drawing magic, as I did. And, the skill with which he carved the new fetish could not be dismissed.

Thinking back on the time we'd spent together, it was clear that we'd grown close. There had been a lot going on in a very short time, and we'd come to depend on each other for what we would need to achieve. I absolutely admit that in another time and under different circumstances, I could very well see myself falling for Alex. I think he might have had some feelings towards me. There were instances I could recall - a touch of his hand, the tone of his voice, the look in his eyes. It was easy to imagine being with him in a romantic relationship. Whatever that potential, however, it was unlikely to happen. There was still a demon to vanquish, and even if we were successful, Alex and his associates still had an inter-planal leak to fix.

I stretched and felt Alex move beside me. He turned to look at me and smiled. "Good..." he looked around for the clock, "whatever time of the day it is...morning, maybe?"

The clock read 10:28. I wasn't sure what time we'd made it to bed, but we'd probably slept for at least 10 hours. "How are you feeling?"

"Mmmmmmm," he said. "A bit achy, actually. My knees are not very happy with me."

"Are you...OK with what we did? You don't feel weird about it or anything?"

"No. Not at all." He raised a hand to draw his finger across my cheek. "I have absolutely no regrets. It was... intense, wasn't it? It was almost like I was losing my virginity all over again. Only this time, to a more experienced, older woman." As soon as the last word left his lips, his eyes flew wide. "Not — not that you are an older woman!" he sputtered.

I laughed out loud and he visibly relaxed, the smile returning to his face.

"Actually," he said, "if we're being honest, had I not become a time traveler - and notwithstanding the fact that I'd be dead - I am obscenely older than you."

I felt that, given the intensity of our coming together, we needed to speak about it. I wanted to hear it from him that he'd felt the same level of desire I had. "Alex, last night —"

There was a quiet tapping on the door then. "You guys awake yet?" Brighid asked. "I thought I heard voices."

Instinctively, I gathered the sheets up around me, covering up my nakedness.

I saw a smirk on Alex's face as he swung his legs over the side of the bed, grabbed a towel off the floor and wrapped it around his waist. "We'll talk later," he smiled. He opened the door a crack.

Brighid peered in. I saw her eyes widen when she realized I was naked. Surely she'd understood what we'd been up to within the ritual. Oh, but then she probably wouldn't have expected to find us still naked in bed together unless we were... Oh, boy.

"Hey," I said. "We're up. Um. Is there any coffee?"

Brighid smiled. "I'll put some on." She practically skipped back down the hallway. I could tell I was going to have some explaining to do.

We got dressed and made our way out into the living room. Pip looked up from his perch on the sofa. He didn't look best pleased. I must have closed the door to the bedroom before he had a chance to come in last night. Brighid had put the coffee on and it smelled like heaven.

"You guys want something to eat?" She was rummaging in the fridge. "I think you've got some bacon and eggs left."

"How about I go fetch us something from the cafe," Alex said. He glanced at me and winked. What a guy - he was clearing off so I could have a private talk with Brighid about what had transpired over the last day.

"That would be wonderful," I said. "That way we don't have to bother with cooking and cleaning up. Lots of stuff to do…"

Brighid looked at us with narrowed eyes but didn't say anything. Alex downed half a cup of coffee and set out to find breakfast. I closed the door after him and turned back to Brighid. She was grinning like a madwoman.

"You spent the night with him," she sang, doing a little jig for good measure.

"It's not what you're thinking," I said. "We just fell into bed, exhausted, after the ritual. Nothing happened in that bedroom."

"But you were naaaaaaaaa-ked!"

"Witch, please. Calm down. Nothing happened." I couldn't help but smile at her enthusiasm, though.

She frowned at me. "I can't believe you, woman - he's perfect! How could you not go for it?!"

"Well, mainly because we were nearly dead!" I said, shaking my head at her. "See how frisky you feel after hours and hours of intense ritual! How long were we in there, anyway?"

"You were already at it when I got up around 8:30, and were still in there when I fell asleep on the sofa sometime around 9 p.m. or so."

"9? That's early for you."

"Yeah, well - when Alex is back I'll tell you all about it. But, I want to know what happened with you guys!"

I told her about the double ritual, including the sex magic involved, but I stopped short of sharing my emotional reactions. I still wasn't sure how I felt about it, and until I'd come to terms with it myself, I didn't need Brighid's analysis.

"So, it worked? You replaced the fetish?"

"Yes. It should be just as strong as the original, maybe stronger."

"Wow. Mora, I'm impressed. That's some serious magic. I feel even more confident about your trap now." I looked down at the floor. "What? What's wrong?"

I pulled out one of the dining chairs and sat down on it. "Yeah, it was some serious magic. It took a lot out of me, Brighid. I was channeling not just for myself, but for Alex as well. I'm drained."

"So, you can rest today - we have time, yet."

"No, it's not that easy. I mean my magic is drained. I don't know how long it will take me to recharge. My trap may be weakened because I am weakened. It doesn't matter how solid my spell is - if I'm too weak to pull down sufficient power..." I trailed off. I didn't want to think about what it would mean if we failed.

"Oh, Mora," she crossed to kneel in front of me, pulling me into a hug. "I'm sorry. There must be something we can do. Maybe there's something I can do - some sort of magic transfusion or something?"

I laughed at that. "Now that would be something." I pushed her back to look her in the eye. "But, you might get your wish to help, after all." She started to smile. "Don't get excited. If there is any way I can keep you away from that incubus when it comes to it, I will. But, I may have to let you help."

She couldn't help herself smiling, it seemed. "Mora, you know I WANT to help. In any way I can. I know you want to keep me safe, but if I can participate, I'm sure it will only strengthen the working. And I know how dangerous it is. I get it, really, I do."

I kissed her forehead. "You know how much I love you," I said. "I promise to try not to be worried about you."

"Don't be. I know what we're facing. I know how important this is. I promise I will not take any of this lightly." I looked into her eyes. She really meant it. Even if she were excited to be involved, it was clear that she really did understand what was at stake. Pride and fear warred within me. I was going to worry anyway, but at least I could take heart in her growing strength.

Alex came back with the breakfast at that moment. Brighid stood up and headed back into the kitchen. "You guys sit - I'll bring the coffee and stuff." Alex caught my eye as he sat, putting the bags of food on the table. Seeing the question in his eyes, I gave him a small nod, letting him know I'd filled Brighid in on...everything.

Once we settled and started in on breakfast, Brighid gave us the news of what we'd missed while we were doing the ritual.

"We got attacked again." Simple as that. It was almost disconcerting how nonchalant she seemed about it.

"Are you OK?!" I nearly dropped my fork.

"Yeah, yeah, we handled it." She had a sense of pride about it, but I could tell from her steady gaze that she didn't take what had happened lightly. "It happened just after sundown. It started with about twenty or so imps and other types of lesser demons. Fireballs again, but I'd laid an anti-fire spell on the property outside - I hope you don't mind, Mora. I thought of it while you were in the ritual room, and didn't want to interrupt to ask permission - figured it was better to ask forgiveness - anyway, that helped immensely in keeping down the damage. Lingus and Adaine and I were holding our own, but other nature Daemons actually appeared to help us! There were about five of them, I think - it was hard to tell for certain in all the hubbub."

"I never heard anything," I said. Alex shook his head, too.

"Well, you were otherwise occupied," she said with a twinkle in her eye. Alex ducked his head down to fiercely study his breakfast. I'm pretty sure there was a pink hue to his cheeks. "It went on for a couple of hours, the demons coming and going in waves. As soon as we wore out one group, another seemed to take their place. Eventually, they left us alone."

"Are Lingus and Adaine OK?" I asked. I'd go and see them as soon as we finished breakfast.

"Yeah, they're fine. None of us was hurt, thankfully. Lingus thinks it was another warning. That they felt your magic and were trying to disrupt it." She sipped her coffee.

"Wow. I'm sorry Brighid. When I left my note, I really didn't expect that would happen. Thank you for protecting us."

She leaned across the table and squeezed my hand, smiling. "Hey, it's good practice for me." She said it lightly, but I knew it had been a trial for her.

"We've got a bit of a problem though."

"What sort of a problem?" Alex asked.

Brighid chewed her lip. "I think it might be better for Lingus to tell you."

Chapter Nine

We went down to the garden after we'd finished breakfast. Lingus was there, looking as if he had been expecting us. I surmised Adaine might be away again on incubus watch. "How did your ritual go?" he asked.

"We were successful," Alex said. "Morgaine is a wonder." He smiled at me. Then Brighid caught my eye and gave me the eyebrow equivalent of "thumbs up". I felt my cheeks flush.

"Thank you for defending us again," I said. "I'm so sorry that happened."

"You have nothing to be sorry for," he said. He came to sit on the ground near the patio while we took our places in the seats there. "It is to be expected that the demons would try to disrupt your working. I am pleased to say that Brighid was instrumental in our success. Her anti-fire spell gave us quite an advantage."

"Brighid said you had some help from other Daemons this time. Will we have their support now?"

He took a deep breath before continuing. "There is some difficulty there. The Daemons are watching, yes. And, they are supportive of our efforts."

"But, they don't wish to involve themselves further?" Alex asked.

"It is not quite that simple," Lingus said. His fingers worried the hem of his tunic. "They believe one of us is treating with the incubus."

"What?!" I couldn't believe it. "How could they think that? We're trying to get rid of the incubus."

"What troubles them is how the lesser demons found us so readily. The lesser demons are likely being directed in their actions by the incubus, which suggests he has discovered us."

"But, that doesn't mean one of us is allied with the incubus," Brighid said.

I nodded. "We don't know for sure that he didn't track us after the incident at the Salt Air the other night. Just because he didn't follow doesn't mean he didn't somehow put a tracking hex on one of us."

Lingus held up a hand. "I know this. But, at that time, he was still considerably weakened, which makes it unlikely he was able to track you. And there is still the question of how they were able to breach your protective wards. Not just once, but twice."

I glanced at Brighid. She was staring at the ground. "They think it's me, don't they? Because he was so nearly successful in seducing me."

"WE know it isn't you, Brighid," I said. "You haven't been out of our sight since that night."

Lingus nodded. "They didn't speculate on who might be in league with the incubus. In fact, Eryn - who seems to be leading this group - wasn't convinced that the collusion was a conscious one."

"What?" I said, "they think one of us is under some sort of spell? That we're helping the incubus without realizing it?"

"Eryn only put that forth as a possibility," Lingus said. "But the result is that they are hesitant to come forward to help until they are sure that none of us is aiding the incubus."

"Us?" Alex turned to Lingus. "Are you and Adaine suspects, as well?"

Lingus nodded. "Yes. I am afraid so."

"Where is Adaine?" I asked.

Lingus met my eyes, and his widened slightly. "Watching the incubus."

I'd found a hooded fleece for Lingus. We looked like three adults and an adolescent strolling along the beach, if you didn't look too closely. Luckily, there were very few people about today, and no one who was around seemed interested in us at all. Brighid had cast a spell of misdirection which seemed to be working wonderfully. Except on animals.

"Oof," Lingus said, as yet another dog leaped up to lick his face. Every dog we passed loped over to greet Lingus. The spell still worked on the dogs' people though and they took little notice of us, their attention seeming to drift away when their dogs dashed off so they never noticed the brief absence.

Lingus had suggested we seek out Adaine. It was likely that the incubus was inactive as it was daytime. His best chance of catching prey was at night, in the bars, where alcohol and lowered inhibitions would give him an advantage. For my part, I completely trusted Lingus. And I'd had no reason to distrust Adaine - he'd fought just as hard as any of us in our first encounter with the lesser demons, and Brighid said he'd acquitted himself well in the second attack. And, he was like Lingus in some ways - seemingly gentle, polite. I wondered if every one of this branch of the Fae were that gentle. But we needed to know for sure.

Before we'd set off, I'd had time to have a quick word with Alex and Brighid.

"Do either of you think it's Adaine?"

They both looked at each other before Brighid spoke. "I don't know. He seems so…polite."

"Mmm," Alex nodded, "polite, yes. But, Lingus is more…genuinely *kind*." *Polite*. That appeared to be the word we all associated with Adaine. But, for me, polite and kind are not synonymous. Anyone can be polite when the situation warrants regardless of how you actually feel about someone, but being kind is much more - it implies a sense of understanding and caring. I realized I didn't feel that *kindness* from Adaine like I did from Lingus.

"I can not imagine Lingus betraying us," Alex continued, "but I think I probably trust Adaine only because Lingus seems to trust him."

I nodded in agreement with their assessments. "Yes, exactly. Except it seems like Lingus isn't so sure now."

The sun was warm as it beat down on us at midday. I'd put on a light fleece, and was almost over-warm. We had driven to the public access closest to where the incubus was making his lair off the coast. It wasn't far from my place, but not quite comfortable walking distance, at least not with me still feeling like I'd been hit by a truck after the intense ritual. We made our way down the shoreline until we came to an area of the town that was sparsely populated, and was a fair walk from the nearest public access. It was one of the areas where there was a thinning of the island, and nothing much was developed between the seashore and the inland sound. A buildup of the sand dunes obscured the view of the road that snaked along between towns. Beyond the road would be soft sands leading to the inland sound and nature refuge. Perfect place for a demon to come and go unnoticed.

As we walked toward the place the incubus had chosen for its lair, Adaine appeared from a verge of sea grass. We were probably a quarter of a mile's walk from where the sand bar would be located. Adaine seemed surprised to see us. "Is there trouble at the humans' abode?" he asked.

"No," Lingus answered. "We have come to see how things go here." We'd made an agreement to let Lingus talk with Adaine. We didn't want to accuse him. If we were wrong, he might refuse to help us then. For all we knew, there was another agent of the incubus who'd been following Adaine without his suspecting.

Adaine smiled and approached us. "All is quiet at this time. The demon has been aground since the early morning hours."

"Is he fully recovered?" Lingus stepped in front of us then, putting himself between us and Adaine.

"No, but he is strengthening apace. I regret to say he was successful in his hunt last night." Adaine pursed his lips solemnly and lowered his head.

I looked at Alex and Brighid. Their stricken faces reflected my own feelings. "Is she…" I couldn't finish the thought.

"She yet lives," Adaine said. "The incubus only engaged her in what I believe humans refer to as 'making out'."

Lingus looked over his shoulder toward us. "There is some hope. As the incubus is still not at full strength, the victim may still be able to resist him somewhat. She may have had enough of her own will about her to keep the situation from advancing too far."

"But he will have gained strength in the encounter," Adaine said. "It means, however, that your squall is no longer effective. The lady did not dismiss the incubus' advances outright."

Lingus nodded and looked at me. "We will need to prepare for the inevitable."

I nodded. The likelihood of my having time to recover my full magical strength before the deciding encounter was looking less and less likely.

Lingus turned his attention back to Adaine. "Eryn is concerned that someone is helping the incubus."

Adaine received the news with measured calm. He looked at each of us - us humans, that is. "I see." His tone was accusatory. The hairs on the back of my neck stood on end. "You must acknowledge the possibility that one of the humans was compromised in the event at the pleasure den several days ago." This was directed at Lingus.

"The possibility has been noted, yes." Lingus said.

Adaine graced us with a smug smile. "You may not even be aware of your treachery."

I took a deep breath, ready to verbally tear him to shreds, but Alex grabbed my hand, entwining his fingers in mine, staying my temper. Lingus seemed to sense my tension as well, and turned to give me a pointed look. A look that said, *"I will handle this."*

Lingus turned his gaze back to Adaine. "There is, however, the fact that none of the humans has been out of my sight long enough to treat with the incubus since that night. As you know, while you have followed the incubus, I have remained in the garden at Morgaine's, privy to any of the comings and goings of the humans."

"The connection could be psychic, not physical," Adaine said. He looked at the three of us again. "If I had to guess, I might suspect that the flame-haired human has been compromised. She was longest in his presence."

I cut my eyes over to Brighid. To my amazement she didn't say anything. She wasn't even looking at him. She was looking beyond him. I followed her gaze. In the verge of sea grass covering a nearby dune a few hundred feet from where Adaine had emerged, several other figures had come forward. More of the nature Daemons. All were alike enough to mark them as being the same species but like humans, each had differing features, likely indicating the aspect of nature they were attuned to. Standing slightly apart from the rest, nearest to us, was a female Daemon. I presumed this to be Eryn. Fair-skinned with nearly white hair drawn up in wrapped braids, she had a regal bearing, standing straight and wielding an engraved staff that looked more ornamental than utilitarian. The Daemons were watching the proceedings with interest. I suspected they had been watching Adaine for a while.

I glanced at Lingus. I wasn't sure if he were aware of the watchers. He continued to look levelly at Adaine. "It would seem to make sense that Brighid is the most likely human to have been enlisted to aid the incubus," he said. "Except for the fact that he was not even at a strength to sense she was a witch at that time, nor would he have been aware that anyone knew of his true nature and would pose a threat."

Adaine started to look a bit nervous. He squared his shoulders. "Surely, you would not presume to accuse me —"

"Oh, but I would," Lingus said. "You, of all of us, have had the most chances to engage with the incubus." The watchers began to move toward us, silently. If Lingus noticed them, he gave no sign. Alex, Brighid and I couldn't help but stare at them, wondering what they would do.

Adaine noticed our gazes and turned to look behind him. He then faced us again. "I suppose there is no use in denying it any longer. Yes, I have been in contact with the incubus."

Lingus turned and took a step toward us. He looked saddened. I could tell he'd really hoped Adaine hadn't been deceiving us. The other Daemons moved closer, forming a semi-circle behind Adaine.

"They are a disease upon this world," Adaine said, gesturing to the three humans present. "The demons would rid us of them."

Lingus looked startled and rounded on him. "You surely don't believe the demons bear any good will toward us?"

Adaine shook his head, a feverish look in his eyes. "Don't you understand? With demons now entering this plane, they can set the balance of nature to rights again. When the humans are gone, nature can restore itself to dominance."

The lady Daemon spoke then. "You can not truly believe that." She stepped toward Adaine. "The demons do not revere nature. Their plane is one of chaos and desolation. They would make it so here, on this plane, as well. The guardians and others of the Fae would perish before nature could ever hope to reassert itself."

"No!" Adaine spun to face her. "He told me that once the demons destroy the human race, nature can rule the Earth once more. No more of their raping the mother for her resources to waste on their 'comforts'! Don't you see, Eryn? He has begun the restoration!" Well, any question I may have had about what Adaine thought of climate change and humans' role in it was answered.

"How?" Eryn shook her head. "What restoration?"

"As he regains his strength, he grooms his prey to prepare them to incubate his offspring. He will mate with the females, and raise an army of half-demons to rid the world of the vermin of humanity."

"What?!" I stepped toward Adaine. Alex, still holding my hand, gripped it tighter, preventing me from getting too close. Lingus held up a hand, begging my patience.

"He will not destroy his prey?" Lingus asked.

"He only takes what he would for strength." Adaine replied. "This first one will be ready to mate with him soon. She ovulates within the next 48 hours. He will find more females in the coming days. Each will bear as many of his offspring as their bodies will allow. All the while, he will build his strength." He turned to me then. "He will defeat you, witch," he spat. "No matter that I did not get the chance to properly examine your proposed spell before the imps came. You are no match for such as he."

"Enough!" Eryn fixed Adaine with a hard stare. "Adaine, Guardian of the Wilds," she began, raising her arms and calling her magic. "I bind you. I bind you from doing harm to others. Return to the Source and face your judgment."

"No!" Adaine spun and threw his arms up, a fireball forming between his hands.

The rest of the nature Daemons, including Lingus, joined in then. "Adaine, Guardian of the Wilds, we bind you. We bind you from doing harm to others. Return to the Source and face your judgment."

Adaine continued protest, but he was overwhelmed by the strength of the assembled Daemons. A glowing bubble formed around him, shrinking closer and closer to him, eventually it, and Adaine, disappeared with a loud pop taking Adaine, presumably, back to the "Source".

All of the Daemons looked down then, as if praying. They seemed to be in mourning for Adaine as if he had died. Alex, Brighid, and I drew closer together and waited in silence. We were content to take our lead from Lingus as to what to do next. Eventually, all of the Daemons looked up, their mourning finished. Lingus turned to face us.

"I am sorry, Morgaine."

"It's not your fault, Lingus."

"I must accept some responsibility," he said. "I called, and he answered."

Eryn placed a hand on his shoulder. "It could have been any of us, Lingus. You bear no responsibility."

Lingus closed his eyes and bowed his head. "Thank you, Lady."

Eryn stepped to stand beside him and smiled at me. "We regret the deception of our brother."

I nodded. It wasn't entirely an apology, but then I wouldn't expect her to be responsible for all of the Fae.

"How could Adaine think he would get any good will from a demon?" Alex asked.

Eryn shrugged. "I would blame it on his youth, but he is not much younger than me. Perhaps he feels the Earth's pain and thought the demons really meant to help nature."

Brighid stepped forward. "You don't believe the demons taking over would be a good thing?"

"Of course not," Eryn said. "They would seek only to create their world on this plane. They would destroy the human population, but in doing so would have no regard for any damage caused to nature in the process. If anything, the demons would have more in common with humans than we would." She shrugged, "I mean no disrespect, but there are many amongst your kind who harbor as little regard for nature as demons do."

I nodded, "I know. No offense taken."

"We have, with the exception of Lingus, opted to remain neutral in the matter," Eryn said. "But now, I pledge that we," she looked around at her companions who nodded in answer to her unvoiced question, "shall aid you when the time comes."

"Thank you," I said. "We can use all the help we can get."

"I can not promise any help beyond ours," she said, "there may be others among us who would be as easily deceived as Adaine was. But we will spread the word, and encourage others of our kind to rise against the demon."

Alex gave her a small bow. "We appreciate any help. Thank you."

She returned the bow and she and her companions retreated, disappearing into the sea grass.

We all turned and walked back to the car. No one spoke until we'd got back to my place. After making a pot of tea for us, we resumed our places on the patio. At length, Lingus spoke. "We now understand how the lesser demons were able to breach your protection wards. Adaine, who had been invited into the garden, in turn invited the demons."

"But, they didn't get through the building defenses," Brighid said.

"I'd never invited Adaine into the building," I said. "I never got the chance. He said 'no need to invite me in' before the thought to do so had even fully formed in my mind. I wonder if he realized he'd cut off that avenue of attack at the time."

"Perhaps not," Lingus said. "It is not clear that he was thinking in terms of allying with the demon at that early point. Now that he has been sent away, once we remake the wards we should have no further incursions. But, we are running out of time to stop the incubus."

The rest of the afternoon was spent enforcing the protections on my property and in planning and making preparations for our entrapment of the demon, and before dinner-time, Lingus and Brighid joined me in a meditation, trying to channel some of their own magical strength to me. I don't know how well it worked. I felt a little stronger, but that might have just been me trying to remain optimistic.

We'd resolved to follow the incubus tonight. Hopefully with the combined magics of me, Brighid, and Lingus, we would be able to lay a strong enough squall on it to prevent it taking more prey. Now that we knew its plan, we needed to do all we could to keep people safe while we finished our preparations. We also needed find the incubus' first intended victim.

I placed a vial of greenish liquid on the patio table where we'd all assembled after dinner. "I've mixed a contraceptive potion that should prevent impregnation."

Alex picked up the vial and turned it over in his hand. "How does it work?"

"The potion will cause the incubus' sperm to be destroyed by heightening her body's natural defenses, causing her body to cast off any fertilized eggs."

"I don't know, Mora," Brighid said. "You've taught me that it goes against our creed to spell someone in an invasive manner without their consent."

"I know," I said, taking a deep breath. "And, I have reservations about using this potion. In fact, I hope it won't be needed, or that we'll at least have time to get her consent before using it. Now, this potion," I placed another vial on the table, this one containing a pink liquid, "is a better choice, but it depends on her using conventional contraception. It will ensure the efficacy of the contraception."

Brighid smiled, "A hex resist?"

"Yes," I nodded and smiled, pleased that she'd guessed it. "This doesn't have the same moral issues for us, as it is completely a protective potion."

Alex was looking confused.

"A hex resist protects someone from harmful magical intentions," I said. "If the incubus' prey is on conventional contraception, a hex resist would block any magical intervention from the incubus to negate its effects."

"Then, it would just be a matter of hoping her contraception is strong enough for demon…stuff," Brighid said.

I nodded. "We could also do a ward on her to temporarily strengthen her own natural desire to not get pregnant, which might make her less receptive to the incubus' advances."

"Sooooo," Alex began, "if she isn't on any contraceptive…"

"Then, this potion," I indicated the vial of greenish liquid, "would be a last resort. It would be for her own good, but using it without her consent is very much against our ethics."

"I suppose we have to hope it doesn't come to that," he said.

Eryn had asked one of her trusted companions to aid us in keeping an eye on the incubus. Others had volunteered to help as well so we wound up with a relay system, of sorts. When the incubus left its lair, the watcher would inform another volunteer who would inform yet another volunteer and so on until word reached Lingus. Brighid, Alex, and I were ready when the time came.

Brighid did her own glamour, and helped me with one for me and Alex. Lingus used his powers to reinforce them for us. We'd all decided to be as plain as possible so as not to attract too much attention. I kept my hair mousy, but shorter. Alex got unwashed, dishwater blonde hair and a five o'clock shadow. Brighid tamed her long flaming tresses into a nondescript strawberry-blond bob. I was feeling a little more confident this time than the last, but with the incubus having regained a good measure of its strength, there was more of a chance it would be able to sense witches in the vicinity. My weakened magic would also be a burden. Brighid and Lingus had worked on a misdirection spell to reinforce my new protection ward, but we wouldn't know just how well it would work until we were in the demon's presence. The best we could hope for is that if he did sense the presence of witches, he would be unable to pinpoint exactly which of the humans in the area were the witches.

The three of us humans traveled by car, while Lingus used his own mode of transportation. It seemed the Salt Air was a favorite haunt of the incubus, as we'd been informed that he had gone there first.

"Geez, the place is packed tonight," Brighid said as I pulled into the lot.

"It's live music night and that always draws a crowd."

She nodded. "Oh, yeah. On the one hand, more people works in our favor in misdirecting the demon if he senses witches."

"Mmm," I said. "On the other hand, that's more people to worry about protecting if things go all Pete Tong."

Alex caught my eye in the rear-view mirror, his expression bemused. "That sounds like it should be cockney rhyming slang, but I'm not familiar with that one."

"Yeah, it's a modern one," I said. "Peter Tong is an English DJ - or, radio announcer?" I turned to see if he understood what I meant. He nodded, so I guessed he must be familiar with radios and broadcasting. "His name has sort of become rhyming slang for something going wrong. I picked it up from my cousin from England when she came to visit a couple of years ago."

"Well, I certainly hope things don't 'go all Pete Tong' for us." Alex opened his door and swung his legs out. "The first order of business is to locate "Ian" in the bar and attempt to lay that squall on him."

Once we'd all vacated the car, I pressed the locking button, and we walked over toward the blind spot where Lingus would be waiting. "The best way would be to locate him from outside, away from other people. We don't want anyone taking too much of an interest in what we're up to or to get too interested in Lingus."

Alex nodded. "I'll try to keep people distracted while the three of you locate the demon and do your thing." He smirked. "I'll employ the old 'lost tourist' method."

Brighid smiled. "We have the advantage of your accent, especially when it comes to the ladies. They'll want to help for sure!"

I caught Lingus' eye and he moved toward us. "Now, let's just hope no one comes out of the bar while we're working."

Waiting until there was a lull in traffic, Brighid, Lingus, and I went to stand near the door, peering through the glass in search of "Ian." Alex stood guard.

It didn't take long to find him, he was already hard at work drawing in the ladies. Making sure Brighid and Lingus had spotted him too we joined hands and began, Lingus intoning his spell in his native language, Brighid and I channeling the strength of our combined magic into the working. Brighid was having to pull some extra weight this time, since I was weakened. The more I used my magic, the longer it would take for me to recharge, so I was drawing on it as little as possible. We managed to just finish before a group of rowdy guys, brushing off Alex's request for directions to the nearest four-star hotel, lumbered over to enter the bar. Lingus, wearing the borrowed hoodie, turned and made his way to the hiding spot to watch the doors before the guys spotted him. Alex, Brighid, and I followed them in and made our way over to a corner that allowed us a pretty good view of the entire room.

Chapter Ten

We watched "Ian" for a while. It was like watching a lounge lizard working the room.

"I think Lingus' squall is having some effect," Alex said.

Brighid nodded. "He's still keeping the ladies interested, but none of them seem overly keen."

"He seems to only be affecting women in his immediate presence," I said. "When we were here the other night, before Lingus' first squall, every heterosexual woman in the place was glued to his every movement, and that was when he was weaker." I should know - he very nearly drew me in, as well.

"I'd say this squall is more effective than the first." I patted Brighid on the arm, acknowledging her contribution.

We'd been standing near one of the taller tables on the perimeter. The group sitting there got up to leave, and we grabbed the stools, positioning ourselves so that we all had a good view of the room. A waitress wandered over to clear their clutter and take our orders.

"Hey! Are ya'll new around here?"

"Mmm," I nodded, "just having a night out here for a change - we're from Manteo." Patty, our waitress, had served Brighid and me often. At least our glamours were good enough to fool humans.

"Oh! Well, welcome to the Salt Air! What can I get for you?"

We ordered, and before she could drift away, I thought I'd see if we could find out anything about the lady the incubus had been with last night. "'Scuse me, do you know that guy over there?" I pointed.

"Oh, him," she said, smiling. "I think his name is Ian. He's been in a few times this week. He's quite a looker, isn't he?" She licked her lips and started twirling a strand of hair between her fingers.

"My friend who recommended this place to us mentioned having seen him here last night. I think he bought her a few drinks. She was pretty giddy about it," I had no idea what the girl's name was if the waitress asked. I was only hoping I was baiting the right hook, so to speak.

"Oh, yeah…" she furrowed her brow, "the blonde girl, with glasses? Yeah, I wonder where she is - they were kind of tight last night."

Yes! That was exactly what I wanted. At least now we had a basic description. Nothing too outstanding about it though - who knew how many blonde girls with glasses lived around here, or might be in town having a late vacation. "Hmmm…maybe she'll be in later," I said, mentally channeling the suggestion to the waitress that she would want to alert me if my 'friend' came in.

"Yeah…" the waitress was staring at "Ian", but didn't seem quite as enamored as she had originally. "I'll be right back with your drinks!"

We continued to watch as the incubus made the rounds between groups of women. As soon as he moved away from one group, it seemed his mojo went with him, and the ladies went back to laughing and talking amongst themselves, taking little notice of him. They weren't ignoring him completely, but they didn't seem any more interested in him than they did in any of the other attractive men present. The incubus was starting to notice. And, it was obviously frustrating him.

The band started their set at the same time the waitress returned with the drinks. "Hey!" She shouted at me over the music. "I think your friend's here!" She pointed back toward the door.

We all followed her finger and saw a medium-height blonde girl with glasses, looking a bit distressed. She was scanning the room, and I could guess who she was looking for. When she spotted the incubus, she started making her way through the crowd toward him. He saw her coming, and with a frown, strode toward her and met her near the bar. He was not happy to see her. I got the distinct impression that he hadn't expected her to be here tonight. I wondered if he'd put some sort of spell on her that had been disrupted by Lingus' squall. As he spoke to her, he started turning on the charm again. She relaxed and started smiling and nodding. Then, she turned to go. Only, halfway to the door, a confused expression came over her face and she spun back around to confront him again. He was definitely aware that something wasn't right now. He started looking around the room. We all turned to each other and faked laughing at something when his gaze fell in our direction. I still had a peripheral view of him. He paused only momentarily before continuing to scan the room. Then he started speaking to the blonde again. It seemed he'd abandoned the idea of charming her, for her demeanor didn't relax this time. But, somehow, he seemed to convince her to leave. She started walking toward the door again, and he faded back into the crowd.

"She's leaving!" I said, rummaging in my purse for the potions.

"Here, give them to me," Brighid said. "I recognize her from the library - I'll handle this!" I handed her the potions and she headed toward the blonde, slowly shedding her glamour. As she was on the move, no one seemed to notice the gradual change in her appearance. I kept looking back toward where "Ian" had gone, hoping he didn't spot Brighid. She met the blonde just as she was opening the door, made a "fancy seeing you here" gesture, looped her arm through the blonde's and they were out the door.

"That was close," Alex said. I realized I'd been holding my breath through all of that, and took in a lungful of air.

We continued to observe the incubus. He was agitated. Knowing that something was disrupting his powers, and probably sensing a witchy presence, he stalked from the bar to the dance floor and back again. He scanned the room again. This time, instead of looking past us, his eyes locked on mine. Then they narrowed.

"Oh shit," I said. "Cover's blown!" Alex stood up and moved to put himself between me and the incubus. He didn't come toward us though. He just grinned and slowly nodded. Then, he turned back to the rest of the room. We watched as he walked over to a table with two couples, probably out on a double-date. Instead of charming the women, though, we watched him make a gesture with his hand. One of the guys leaned over and kissed one of the girls. Only, it was apparently not the girl he was with. The other guy stood up, grabbed his friend's collar, and threw a punch. The girls started shouting at each other. The incubus turned to face us, still grinning, and raised his hands in the air. He flicked both wrists. We watched as group after group, couple after couple started fighting. It was soon turning into a bar brawl. Even the band had put down their instruments and were throwing punches at each other. It seemed that since there was a squall on his love mojo, the demon had turned on his hate mojo. Human nature being what it is, even under a squall, the incubus' influence didn't require much power to incite a bar brawl.

Alex and I made our way to the door, ducking and dodging as bodies, bottles, and furniture started flying. A bottle shattered on the wall just above my head, showering me in amber glass and tepid beer. Alex lifted his denim jacket over our heads as we picked our way to the door. The place had completely erupted in fighting. If people weren't throwing punches, they were hurling obscenities at one another. Most were doing both. We managed to make it out the door just before someone got thrown through it. We stumbled out of the way just in time to avoid getting taken down with the guy as he flew through the door behind us. Lingus moved toward us, alarmed.

"He's using hate magic!" I said as we made our way to my car.

"We can not combat that without Brighid and with you weakened," Lingus said. "Best to retreat and regroup."

"My thoughts, exactly," Alex said, opening my door and settling me in the driver's seat. He ran around the car and opened the passenger door. "We'll meet you back at the shop!"

Lingus floated into the air and turned in the direction of my place. I started the car and got us on the road, just before the first of the police cars rounded the corner. Moments later, they would have blocked off the parking lot and we'd have been trapped. Breathing a sigh of relief, I drove us back to the shop. I just hoped Brighid hadn't got caught in any of the fallout.

Alex and I collapsed on the sofa as soon as we got home. In a rare move, Lingus came in with us, although he asked for us to keep the window open as he was more comfortable that way. Not long after we got back, Brighid arrived. She seemed perkier than the rest of us, which I took as a good sign.

"How did it go?" I asked as she joined us on the sofa.

"She's a lovesick puppy," she shrugged. "but, I didn't have to use the green stuff." We all made relieved noises.

"You said you knew her?" I prompted, turning back to Brighid.

"Yeah, it was Paula, from the library," Brighid said. "She helped me with research for writing my business plan a couple of years ago."

"She recognized you, then?" Alex asked.

"She did, but it was a bit awkward, as we are really only acquaintances. She was obviously upset, and I didn't want to seem to be *too* interested, but I didn't want to come across as not caring, either. I wound up saying 'Hey, you look like you could use a drink', and we ended up a few blocks away at that new place near the grocery store. I'd promised to buy, so I sat her down and went up to the bar. Luckily, some goofball was all 'hey, y'all - watch this' with his friends which was enough of a distraction for me to sneak the hex resist potion into her drink. I figured it was best to get that in her at least. Maybe it will help protect her against Ian's mojo in general."

"Did she tell you what happened?" I kicked off my shoes and tucked my feet beneath me.

"Not everything, and I didn't push since we're not really close. She said she'd met a guy the night before and thought he was perfect. Only she hadn't heard from him all day and when she went to the bar hoping to run into him again, things seemed weird."

Lingus nodded, "That might have been our squall taking effect."

"In any event, I played the sympathetic acquaintance, encouraging her to enjoy her bevvy, and telling her things would definitely improve soon. After a while, she loosened up enough that I was able to turn the conversation around to preferred contraceptive methods. I pretended I was having a reaction to the one I was using and asked if she had any recommendations."

I smiled, "Nice one!"

Brighid nodded. "She's on the pill, I'm happy to report. I was able to whisper a ward to increase her reluctance and resistance to getting pregnant, like you'd talked about."

I nodded.

"Then, I got her safely home, and her roommate promised to look after her. As an added bonus, the roommate has had it with Paula's bad luck with men. She said she had half a mind to kick the ass of the next loser who comes sniffing around the apartment, so I warded her with heightened protective desires!"

"You officially rock, Brighid!"

She smiled, "I put a general protective ward on the building, too. Probably best if Ian doesn't 'come sniffing around'. After that, I came here. What the heck did you guys get up to? It's like the whole village has gone mad. The taxi driver kept going on about a brawl at the Salt Air and fights breaking out all over town."

We all looked around at each other. Finally, Alex spoke. "The incubus caught on to the squall. Then, he spotted us, and started using some sort of…what did you call it Morgaine?"

"Hate mojo."

"How'd he catch on to you?"

I shrugged. "As near as I can figure, it was the extra magic around us from Lingus' strengthening of our glamours. Which means he's getting stronger more quickly than we'd like. Anyway, instead of just coming for us, he set the entire bar to fighting. In a way, that might be a good sign - that he's not strong enough yet to confidently take us on."

"Well, he didn't just stop at the Salt Air," Brighid said. "There's trouble all over. Cop cars everywhere. If the taxi driver is to be believed, there was rioting and looting at the liquor store."

I grabbed the remote and turned the television on. Sure enough, our town was all over the local news. Fights and an instance or two of rioting reported throughout the village but, luckily, no major crimes or injuries. The riots only involved about 4-6 people and were quickly contained. It's a small village, so there was definitely some interest in what had made everyone go a bit crazy, but not so much as to warrant having the national guard called out or anything so drastic. Still, the reporter seemed amused by it all, joking about something in the water or full-moon madness, although it was past the peak of the full moon.

I sighed. "I guess we'd better try to diffuse things. Lingus, would you be more comfortable if we did this outside?"

"I think I can manage indoors for a bit, if it's more comfortable for you?"

I nodded. "Alex, will you join us? We could use your energy." I knew he still felt a bit bad about not being able to use skills like the ones that Brighid and I did when it came to defending against the imp attack, though the skills he was allowed were extremely important. Even without active participation, the energy of his good will would certainly be helpful.

"I'd like that," he smiled.

We all moved to the ritual room. In the middle of the circle, I smoothed out the map of the village that we'd been using to track the demon. The four of us sat around it and joined hands. I allowed a moment for Brighid and me to center ourselves and to mentally build the protective magical circle around us. I'd practiced this particular type of ritual with Brighid before as a duet, of sorts. One of us would say a line, then the other.

"Guardians of the East, South, West, and North, we respectfully request your attendance," I began.

Brighid continued, "Enter we now into this circle in perfect love and perfect trust."

In unison, the four of us said, "In perfect love and perfect trust."

"Guardians," I continued, "watch over our work, and guide our intentions to the good of all, harming none."

We sat silently for a few moments, allowing our energies to build.

Then it was Brighid's turn, "Now, we direct our energies onto this village and all who dwell within."

For Alex and Lingus' benefit, I said, "Imagine a dome of shimmering light around the map, and project that outward, to the village around us." I allowed a few moments of silence while we all concentrated on our visualization. "Let peace and well-being descend upon the inhabitants of this village."

Brighid said, "Let tempers be calmed, and let empathy for others arise in the hearts of all who dwell here."

I glanced around the circle and, in unison, we all said, "As we will, so mote it be."

We went back to the living room and turned the television back on. Gradually, the scenes changed from those of angry people and fights to those of people wandering around, looking a bit confused. Eventually those who had been fighting or arguing previously were helping each other with cleaning up debris, or passing around coffee or bottles of water. Very few people seemed to be arguing anymore. The field reporter seemed somewhat disappointed at the turn of events, obviously hoping for the conflict to continue in order to provide more interesting fodder for the evening news.

He stuck a microphone in one woman's face as she passed, carrying a box of doughnuts, nearly bopping her on the nose with it. "Ma'am? Can you tell us what happened? Has everyone been drinking, or doing mushrooms, or something?" He chuckled and winked at the camera, pleased with his little joke.

She shrugged. "I don't know. But whatever it was, I think we're over it now."

"But, surely something made you all start fighting," he persisted. "Can you give us any indication as to what caused this chaos?"

"Well, I don't know if you'd want to call it chaos, exactly. Probably just some misunderstandings. And it's not like everybody in town was involved." She shrugged again, "Anyway, I'm going home after I pass these around." She wandered out of the camera shot leaving the reporter shaking his head. As he engaged in some banter with the on-air anchor, I turned the telly off.

"I've got an idea," I said.

A little over an hour later, Alex, Brighid and I were wandering around the village, placing little bouquets of herbs and flowers here and there. Combining herbs known for their calming and evil-repelling influence with flowers of love and good will from the classic "flower language" of the Victorians, we'd made the small bouquets in the shop before setting out to place them around town. Brighid and I did our witchy thing to further infuse the bouquets with calming and evil-repelling magic, and Alex and Lingus tied them together with brightly colored ribbon. For plants not in season here, Lingus collected them for us from…somewhere.

"Where and how did Lingus get the other plants so quickly?" Brighid asked.

"I didn't ask. He probably wouldn't have told me, anyway." Between my making a list of the ones we'd need, and the time we'd spent gathering what plants I had readily available, he'd had gone and returned with all the other plants.

"Do you think these will work?" Alex asked, as he stretched to tie one of the bouquets high on a lamp post. There were still a few unsettled pockets of humanity in the area. Most of the "hate mojo" the incubus had let loose had dissipated with the help of our little ritual and the likelihood that the demon had gone to ground for the time being, but not everyone had got over it quite yet. And, there was a higher concentration of lesser demon activity. The incubus had obviously called on some friends to fan the flames, so to speak.

"There are several herbs and flowers in these that the lesser demons will avoid, so that should help some," I said, handing him the scissors to trim the twine. "At least it will keep the lesser demons from making things worse, hopefully." It was after midnight now, and very few people were still around. Those who were still out mostly ignored us, continuing to clean up after the fights and presumably expecting we were doing the same.

Brighid pulled her jacket tighter against the autumn chill. "I wonder where Ian is now. Surely he'd want to hang around and enjoy his handiwork."

I'd noticed Alex wince before when she referred to the incubus by the human name he'd taken, and he did so again now. I knew the feeling - far better to think of him as something other than human, since he was. I shrugged. "I don't know. I'd just as soon not run into it again until we're good and ready for him." I glanced around half-expecting to see it lurking in the shadows, laughing at us.

"He's probably gone underground again," Alex said, taking another bouquet from my bag of them and starting off down the street. "While he's obviously quite good with using hate, his speciality is using seduction and taking advantage of feelings of love and desire to feed on. He'll have better luck when things are calm again, I'd wager."

We walked on, stopping to place the bouquets. We wouldn't get to the entire village, it was small, but not small enough to cover in one night, and certainly not on foot. We concentrated on the town center, placing as many of the bouquets as we could near the heaviest areas of people-traffic.

When we got back, we used up the remaining bouquets in the block around my immediate neighborhood. The shops were closed, and there was very rarely any human presence other than me in the area after store hours, but anything to help deter attacks on us by the lesser demons was a good thing.

Lingus was waiting for us in the garden when we returned to the shop. He had a guest with him. Eryn, the lady guardian stood with him near the patio.

Lingus raised a hand in greeting. "There is news," he said simply. He gestured toward the patio seats and we took our places. He and Eryn sat on the grass at the edge of the patio.

Eryn, sitting in a lotus position, leaned forward placing her elbows on her knees and resting her fingertips on the ground. "The incubus has left this plane."

"What?" I sat forward so quickly I nearly toppled off the seat. I looked over at Alex. "It can't have been that easy."

"No," Lingus said. "The incubus left of his own volition. Our attempts to thwart him have been nothing but a minor irritant, I'm afraid."

"We surmise, given what we have overheard amongst the lesser demons, that he has returned to his own plane to more quickly regain his strength." Eryn gave me a sad smile. "I fear this will make your task more difficult, should he return at his fullest strength."

I sighed. *Great, just what I needed to hear.* "But, he'll be weakened again when he makes the crossing, won't he?"

Alex laid his hand over mine, where it rested on the arm of the chair. "Yes, but not as weak as he has been. Remember, we got lucky with his original crossing being during Samhain. This time, there will not be the concentration of benevolent spirits to harry him."

"Mora, you've got me to help, too, remember?" Brighid gave me her most hopeful smile.

Yeah, I've got you to worry about, I thought. Even though I knew Brighid knew the stakes, and was taking this very seriously, and truly wanted to help. Even though I trusted her, and believed in her strengths, she was my dear friend and almost like a little sister in some respects. I was going to worry about her no matter what, and even more so if the incubus was stronger. I feared my worry for her would compromise me.

"Yeah," I said smiling and nodding at her, hoping I was successful in hiding my reservations from her. "I got you, babe." She laughed at that and leaned across to hug me. I held her tightly and bit back the sudden rush of emotion threatening to spill out.

"I don't suppose Ian will just find somewhere else to go when he comes back, instead of coming here?" Brighid looked at Lingus and Eryn.

"He will most likely return here. He's become familiar with the area and its inhabitants, and has laid the groundwork for his plans here," Eryn said.

"And," Lingus added, "I suspect at this point, it's become personal."

"Well," Alex said, clapping his hands together, "I suggest we make the most of this reprieve." *Reprieve?* We all turned to look at him as if he'd gone mad. He looked back at each of us. "What? I'm not suggesting we go on holiday! There is nothing to be done about it, if the demon isn't on this plane. The best thing for us to do is to be as ready for his return as we possibly can." We all nodded at that.

"That would be the wisest course of action," Lingus said.

Eryn stood and brushed her tunic off. "I agree. I will coordinate with our people so all understand what is at risk. Perhaps we may be able to encourage more of us to help our human friends." She smiled warmly at us. "Morgaine, the best thing for you to do is to rest as much as you can and recover your own strength." To my questioning expression she said, "Lingus explained the sacrifice you made to restore Alex's carving. You are very brave. I know your instinct is to *do*. To do something, anything. But you should rely on your friends for a time. Let them help. Let them *do*. Calm yourself. Center yourself. Rest. That is the best way to recharge your magic." With that she turned, her wings unfurling in a sparkling wave, and floated gracefully into the sky and away.

Chapter Eleven

ryn's advice was easier said than done. It had been just over a week since we'd learned the incubus had retreated to its own plane. I hadn't been able to really rest, never knowing when the excrement might make contact with the electric-powered oscillating air shifting device, so to speak. Our bouquets seemed to be doing the trick at keeping the peace and deterring the lesser demons, thanks to the spell keeping them from wilting. We'd noticed that tempers were still short however, so some of the incubus' "hate mojo" must still making the rounds. I kept poking at my notes, reading through the Ænigmata books, my book of shadows, Brighid's notes, looking for anything that might strengthen our chances against a stronger incubus. All I got for my trouble was a headache and a telling off when Brighid found me with my nose in the books again.

"Do you want us to fail?!" she said, hands on her hips, green eyes flashing, ginger tresses blowing wildly behind her (despite the lack of natural wind).

From my spot on the floor of the ritual room where I'd spread all our notes, maps, diagrams and books, I looked up at her, admiring her command of the nature magic providing her with the breeze. "I'm not doing anything strenuous!" I protested.

She shook her head and walked over to me, grabbing my arm and pulling me up, releasing the wind spell. "Part of your recovery is going to depend on a quiet mind. This," she indicated the mess on the floor, "isn't providing you with a quiet mind."

Alex poked his head into the room, obviously drawn by the commotion. "She's right, you know." Though he was here every day, he'd moved to a closer hotel, and wasn't staying overnight for the time being. Brighid thought he should be - and had made her thoughts on that perfectly clear to me - and I admit I kind of wish he was staying around day and night. I didn't examine my own reasons too closely. I wasn't sure I was ready for what I might find. We'd had yet to find time for a serious talk about...things.

"I thought you were on my side," I admonished him. He just shrugged.

Brighid gave my shoulders a shake and caught my eye. "Remember when you were teaching me about meditation and you told me something very wise that you said applied to meditating and often to other aspects of life? 'Sometimes you have to stop looking for the answers and let them find you'."

"Yeah, y'know…I'm pretty sure I didn't invent that line."

"Doesn't matter. I'm asking you to take your own advice."

I grimaced.

"Not easy is it?" She looped her arm through mine and pulled me out of the room and down the hall. When we got to the living room, she sat me on the sofa and handed me a "Sandman" comic. "Read this. Then, you're having a nap. I'll go over our notes again later —" she held her hand up as I opened my mouth to speak, "— I'll keep my nose out of the naughty books." She knew I wasn't fond of the idea of her perusing the Ænigmata. Hell, I didn't really like reading them. And anyway, I'd probably got as much out of them as was possible.

"Yes, mother," I shook my head, defeated. She was right, of course. No one likes feeling helpless. Now I got a taste of how Alex felt when he couldn't use magic to help us with the lesser demon attack. I couldn't imagine having to choose between being a witch and only being allowed certain aspects of magic, even if it was very important magic. I looked over at Alex, who was watching me. The hint of an understanding smile he gave me made me think he might have known what I was thinking.

As she headed toward the door leading down to the shop, Brighid said to Alex, "You stay here. Make sure she rests!" He jumped to attention and gave her a curt nod. Brighid had insisted on helping out in the shop while I "rested" and Alex had been dividing his time here during the day between the shop and the flat, helping with stocking and moving things around for Brighid, keeping his tools prepped and doing some reading of his own from my library. I tried not to think of what sorts of conversations those two might have been having about me. I'd asked Brighid not to lay on the "wing-lady" routine too thickly.

Pip hopped down from next to me on the sofa and gave a languorous stretch before strolling closer to the window and flopping down in a sunbeam. Alex came over and took Pip's place, turning toward me and propping one knee up in the space between us. He reached out and took both of my hands, and I shifted my position to face him. "How are you feeling, really?" he said.

I let out a frustrated sigh. "Helpless. I feel like I should be doing more." I looked into his eyes. The way he looked at me...it was like he was seeing into my soul, and inviting me to peer into his. I smiled sadly. "Scared, too. What if I'm not —"

"Shhh," he shook his head. "Worrying that you won't get your magical strength back won't help, you know."

"I know, I know. But, I can't seem to stop."

He wrinkled his brow, looking thoughtful. "What you need is a distraction."

"What kind of distraction?" I said. Unbidden, my mind brought up a remembrance of the ritual, and I felt my face flush.

He looked at me, his eyebrows raised. "Ah…" he said, and smiled, obviously picking up on my train of thought. Then cleared his throat. "Well, actually, I was thinking of something like…Oh! It's your Thanksgiving next Thursday, isn't it? Perhaps you can show me what this Thanksgiving thing is all about?"

I pulled my hands away and glared at him. "You want me to make like a 'good little woman' and cook Thanksgiving dinner for you?! How is that supposed to help me relax?"

He realized his error and started sputtering. "No! I didn't mean —"

I laughed then. "You are so cute when you're discombobulated!" I felt like a teenager, flirting with the school science club president (I never went in for the jock types - I was always more drawn to brains than brawn).

He gave me a stern look then. "Miss Morgaine, if I didn't know any better I'd say you're getting your sense of humor back."

"I wasn't aware I'd lost it!"

He reached for my hands again. "You have been a bit tense lately, but it's understandable. Why don't we plan a Thanksgiving picnic - together?"

I favored him with a smile. "Yeah. That'd be nice."

He smiled and leaned in a bit. "Morgaine, we haven't had a chance to discuss how things stand with us since the ritual. And, I know you said I was welcome to stay here instead of wasting money on a hotel room, but… well, it's just… I mean, I just wanted to say that —"

Just then, we heard Brighid running up the stairs and the door popped open. Such awful timing! Alex and I really needed to have this conversation about things between us. I knew I was attracted to Alex. After the ritual I was certain he'd stolen my heart. I had a reasonable suspicion that he felt the same about me. I think he might have been just about to tell me that. But, it looked like any personal conversation would have to wait. Again.

Brighid gave me an apologetic look. "Um, Mora…I think you'd better come down."

Alex and I traded concerned glances and got up to follow her back down to the shop. When we reached the store room, I could hear a commotion outside coming from the direction of the front of the shop. Sure enough, when we reached the shop door I could see the cause of the noise, standing on the sidewalk over the road.

"Oh, fuuu-crying tears in the sink!" I said. Five ladies in their mid 50s to early 60s stood defiantly, holding signs and shouting. As we watched, one of them - quite obviously the one in charge, her salon-blond hair perfectly coiffed, and dressed like she'd just stepped out of the Carlisle Collection trunk show catalog - hurled one of our bouquets toward the shop. It splatted and broke apart as it hit the door. Other bouquets were littered about on the ground and road, having been thrown down and stomped on, or crushed under the wheels of the infrequent car traffic.

"No more devil's work! No more devil's work!" "Get right with Jesus! Get right with Jesus!" "Witchcraft is an abomination!" "Exodus 22:18!" "Leviticus 19:31!" "Leviticus 20:6!" "Leviticus 20:27!" were among the phrases they were shouting, or had written on their signs.

"Who is that?" Alex asked.

"That," said Brighid, "is Mrs. Celia Davidson. Local fundamentalist busybody." She spat the last bit out like it was spoiled fruit.

"Now, Brighid," I began, but then flinched as another bouquet splattered against the door. I looked back out at the group. Celia was winding up for another bouquet toss. "Celia certainly is in a mood. If I had to guess, I'd say she'd had a full dose of the incubus' 'hate mojo' - and liked it."

"And, she's brought minions, it would seem," Alex said. He seemed a little more amused than was necessary. "Looks as if they know their Leviticus."

"Not all of it," Brighid said.

"Huh?"

Brighid winked at him. "I'll explain later."

I shook my head and reached for the door. "Well, I suppose there's nothing else for it."

Alex and Brighid followed me as I stepped out of the door. Celia started shouting louder as the three of us faced the five of them across the beach road. It was a shame that the beautiful view of the sea from here was disrupted by the hateful signs the women bore, and the peaceful susurrus of the waves drowned out by their belligerent shouting.

There are parking areas on the other side of the block from us, inland from the beach road. Though most people park there and the beach road is almost always only filled by foot traffic even during peak season, the occasional car does travel this way. Therefore, I looked left and right before stepping out into the road. As we crossed toward the protesters I clasped my hands demurely in front of me, attempting to project a calm, inoffensive demeanor. Celia and I were never going to be friends or see things eye to eye, but it is just my nature to be polite to people, even if I don't particularly like them. And, it would be worth the effort if it would defuse this situation. I wasn't concerned with the other ladies - two of them were regular customers, anyway - but, I knew them all to be a bit in awe of Celia, and they tended to go along with whatever she wanted.

"Mrs. Davidson," I said with a placating smile, stepping onto the sidewalk in front of her. "I sense you are unhappy with me."

Celia drew herself up to her full height of 5' 5" and fixed me with her steeliest glare. "You'd best not have any ideas about trying to hex me, Morgaine Clemenson. I've got God on my side!" Some of her posse murmured some quiet 'Amens'.

"Mrs. Davidson, I have no intention of 'hexing' you. I couldn't even if I wanted to - it would only reflect back on me."

"And the Lord God will send your evil back upon you threefold, heathen!"

I almost laughed. Celia had no idea how close she was to the truth of the threefold law of return. "Please, believe me, I wish you no ill-will." I kept my expression placid and tilted my head slightly to the side. "Would you please tell me what I have done to make you so angry?"

She grabbed one of the few intact bouquets at her feet and shook it in my face. "Why don't *you* tell me what sort of putrescence you mean to spread amongst us with these devices of Satan?"

I calmly took the bouquet from her. "These are floral and herbal bouquets, Mrs. Davidson. What makes you think there is anything evil about them?"

"Because almost two weeks ago, these…things appeared all over town, and all sorts of bad things started happening - fights and looting and people disrespecting each other. Don't you think I don't know Satanic ju-ju when I see it!" Never mind that the "bad things" happened before we made the bouquets, Celia loves nothing more than a conspiracy, and the timing was close enough for her to make one. "And not a one of 'em has started to wilt, and that just isn't natural!"

"Well now, Celia," one of her friends (and one of my regular customers), Elaine Evans, chimed in, "you remember those flowers Sammy gave me for Mother's Day last year? They had some kind of flower food with them that kept them fresh for a really long time." Celia turned the glare on her and Elaine blanched and suddenly became extremely interested in the sand at the edge of the pavement.

"Mrs. Davidson," I said quietly, drawing her attention back to me, "I made these bouquets using Victorian flower language, just like Melissa did with the tussie-mussies she made as wedding favors." I was treading a bit close to the edge bringing Celia's daughter into this, but I knew all of the ladies standing in front of us had been enlisted by Celia to help construct the wedding souvenirs to Melissa's specifications. As I expected, the other ladies made noises of remembrance. "And I used herbs that have calming and soothing properties. I think if you were to ask around, you'd find that the bouquets were placed after the bit of trouble. I only meant to remind everyone to be kind to each other."

Instead of calming her down, my sensible explanation seemed to only further infuriate Celia. She leaned closer and brought her finger up to point at my nose. She was close enough that I could smell the tuna and onions she'd had for lunch as she hissed through gritted teeth, "Now, see here missy. I know you think you're being clever, but I see right through you to that evil black pagan heart of yours. You may think you've got this town under your thumb, but make no mistake, I plan to —"

Just to my left, someone cleared their throat. Celia and I both turned to look. A tall gentleman with thinning white hair and a neatly trimmed beard stood looking down at one of the ruined bouquets, held in his hand. It was the pastor of the local Episcopal church, the Parish Church of St Mary and St Romuald.

Reverend Wilson Carver, affectionately known as "Father Wil", looked up at us. "Morgaine, did you put these up around town?"

I caught Celia's smirk out of the corner of my eye. She obviously thought she was about to get some support in her righteous protest against the local witch.

"I did, Father Wil," I said and indicated Alex and Brighid, who'd been quietly watching the scene unfold. "My friends and I made them and put them out."

"Well, that was very thoughtful of you," he smiled. "After the unpleasantness of that night, it was so nice to see some beauty when I went for my morning walk the next day." I felt Celia's expression fall as much as saw it. I noticed her jaw working as she sought something to say, and so did Father Wil. "Good afternoon, Mrs. Davidson, ladies!" He nodded politely at the assembled protesters.

He made a show of looking over their signs, pursing his lips and furrowing his brow. "Hmmm...you've misspelled 'abomination'...there's no 'b' after the 'm'."

Celia bristled, but keep her voice even. "I hardly think that diminishes the meaning, Reverend."

Father Wil answered without looking at her, continuing to study the signs, "No, but the message is quite harsh."

"Well, the bible, Leviticus especially, is quite clear about witches and witchcraft —"

Father Wil held up a hand to stop her. "I am quite aware of what Leviticus says, Mrs. Davidson. And I feel at this point I need to remind you that Leviticus contains no mention of the terms 'witch' or 'witchcraft'. The very passages you've used here, with the exception of the one from Exodus, do not contain either of those words."

"Well, Leviticus talks of sorcery - same thing!"

"No," Father Wil shook his head, "no mention of sorcery in Leviticus either, although there are several mentions of it in other books of the bible."

Celia huffed, "Well, I hardly see how the semantics of what word is used to describe it makes any difference whatsoever. We all know what it means!"

"Mrs. Davidson," Father Wil began, "I think it would be best if you were to re-familiarize yourself with Leviticus. It would seem you have missed out several important passages, and if you are going to insist on holding to the passages regarding mediums, necromancers, or fortune-tellers, then you should hold to ALL of the passages."

"I'm sure I have no idea what you mean," Celia said. "I read my bible every day and follow my Lord God's commandments!"

"Perhaps," Father Wil said. "But, let me ask you this - your blazer. Is it a blended fabric?"

"It's cashmere and wool, yes." Celia proudly lifted her hand to smooth the collar of her trendy blazer.

"Leviticus Chapter 19 Verse 19 admonishes against wearing clothing of two kinds of material mixed together." Celia's eyes widened. "And, am I right that I saw you at the Sheffield's clam-bake back in the summer? I seem to remember you were particularly fond of the shrimp." Celia nodded, hesitantly. "Well, I'm sorry to tell you that Leviticus Chapter 11 Verse 10 is known to forbid the eating of shellfish."

I heard Brighid whisper to Alex, "That's what I meant by 'not all of it'."

Celia was at a loss for words. I almost felt sorry for her. Almost. Father Wil wasn't being unkind, but I could see she was stung by his words. He was aware of it, too.

"I'm sorry for being a spoilsport," he told her, smiling. "I know you feel very strongly about your convictions and, truly, I admire that. But, I know Morgaine, and I know she isn't an evil person. And, these," he held up the ruined bouquet, "are only flowers."

"Well, perhaps we've been a bit hasty. In this case." Celia, bless her heart, managed to apologize without apologizing. She made a gesture and her friends started gathering their things and folding their signs away.

"I would love for you to attend my next bible workshop," Father Wil said, a wave of his hand indicating all of us. "I think it would prove very enlightening on the subject of just what the bible means and what it doesn't. We will be studying various texts —"

"What various texts?! There's only one true bible!" It seemed Celia wasn't quite ready to go quietly.

"On the contrary, the bible we know today differs considerably from the earliest known Greek translations of the scriptures. There are quite a few passages that we rightly discount in these modern times - things that were reflective of the attitudes of the men setting down translations of scripture in ways that would support the political and social climate of their times." Before Celia could say anything else, Father Wil said, "I'll send you the flier, and you can decide for yourself if it is something that would interest you."

"Well." Celia seemed to have finally decided to retreat. "Ladies, I believe it's time for our book club meeting!"

"But, that was yester—" one of her friends started, and immediately stopped at Celia's sharp look. With that, she and her friends started to leave.

Elaine lagged behind and as she passed by me whispered, "Can you set aside some of your Goat's Milk and Honey bath bars for me for the B & B? I'll be back later in the week. And, um…" she winced, "sorry about all this."

"I do hope I haven't overstepped," Father Wil said, as we watched them leave.

"Not at all!" I said, turning to him. "I'm actually really glad you happened by - I wasn't doing a very good job of talking Celia down, I'm afraid."

"Well, it isn't always easy to reason with the unreasonable," he sighed. "At the risk of sounding hyperbolic, it's Christians like her who give Christianity a bad name."

"Amen to that!" Brighid said.

Father Wil motioned to the shop. "Actually, I didn't just happen by. I've come to to see you."

"Really? How can I help?" I asked as we headed back toward the shop, picking up the debris from Celia's destruction of the bouquets.

"I forgot to tell Chad to put altar candles on the last supply order and we need fresh ones for Sunday services." He gave me a sheepish grin. "I wondered if you might have some beeswax tapers available?" He held the door for us when we got to the shop. "Oh, and as I was coming here anyway, I've also been tasked by our choir director with letting you know that rehearsals for this year's performance of *The Messiah* will start on the Saturday after Thanksgiving."

I wouldn't let Father Wil pay for the candles. Instead I asked if he'd include me and my friends in his prayers.

Alex seemed bemused. "You're a witch, and you've just ask a Christian priest to pray for you."

"Hey - can't hurt, might help!"

"Oh, and you're singing in the choir for the seasonal performance of *The Messiah*." He shook his head. "You're a bit of an enigma, aren't you?"

Brighid giggled. "She used to be a full member of the choir. Every Sunday morning without fail, rocking that cassock and cotta."

I smiled at the memory. "I still fill in from time to time if there's a shortage of altos."

Alex shrugged. "I'm sorry, but it just seems like that's a little unusual for a witch. Don't get me wrong - I'm not judging." He started sifting through the remains of the bouquets, salvaging ones that were still in good shape.

"I don't know," I said. "I'm not really a *religious* person, even within the witching world. But, I do consider myself spiritual, and traditional Christian music is not only some of the most beautiful music in existence, I believe it is, at its core, the highest expression of true spirituality - that is, the emotional connection we feel to this world and to each other." I picked up a sprig of rosemary and twirled it in my fingers. "If I can use my voice to enhance someone's feeling of that true spirituality, I see no conflict with not subscribing to the precepts of that person's particular religion."

Alex had stopped fiddling with the flowers and now looked at me intently, smiling. "You do amaze me, Morgaine."

I tossed the rosemary sprig at him and it stuck in his hair. "Oh, stop it!" I scolded, but smiled at the compliment in spite of myself. "Y'know, you might as well call me Mora. All my best friends do." I smiled at both him and Brighid then. "Let's see if we can recharge some of these bouquets and get them back out around town - the last thing we need is for the lesser demons to have an opening to cause more trouble!"

Chapter Twelve

Having spent most of the afternoon and evening preparing for our Thanksgiving picnic planned for the next day (despite my initial protestations, I wound up volunteering to do most of the cooking), I fell into bed, exhausted. Alex was coming in the morning to help finish up, and Brighid was in Edenton celebrating with her family. It was nice having the place to myself. Things had been fairly quiet since we'd redistributed the bouquets, and as the days went by, the edginess of waiting for the incubus to make a move waned. It helped that I was feeling a little bit stronger magically every day. Pip was usually good about sensing when danger was near, and he was pretty chill lately. It occurred to me that I should have paid more heed to his agitation the evening Adaine arrived. He probably sensed something about Adaine wasn't quite right.

Sometime after midnight, I felt the bed move. At first, I though it was Pip coming or going, but the weight wasn't right. Dragging myself up from the depths of sleep, I opened an eye and peered over to the source of the disturbance. Alex was sliding into bed with me.

"How did —"

"Shhhh…" he said, and dangled a key briefly before setting it on the nightstand. I'd almost forgotten I'd had a key made for him, as he always rang the emergency buzzer when he first arrived if the shop was closed, instead of just using the key. As I noticed he'd stripped already, I imagined he let himself in to surprise me. "I couldn't stay away from you any longer."

I was looking forward to our picnic tomorrow, a chance to spend some time alone and really talk about everything that was happening, but now he was here. "Are you sure?" I asked, as he snuggled up to me, sliding his hand up from my waist and cupping my breast.

"I'm 100% sure. Demons couldn't keep me away from you," he chuckled. He leaned into me, nuzzling my neck and inhaled deeply. "You are delectable!"

A red flag went up then. Something was off. In a flash, my mind replayed the scene at the bar when we went to rescue Brighid - our first encounter with the incubus. He'd grabbed me and pulled me to him, sniffing me. He'd used those very same words. I reached a hand up to his chest, feeling for the raised triskele design of Alex's amulet. It wasn't there. "Wh—where's…"

"Mmm?" he said, kissing the nape of my neck. "Where's what?"

I pushed him away and slid, backwards, out of the bed, backing away, looking around the room. "Cat. Where's my cat?" I looked around. Pip was nowhere to be seen.

"Probably off chasing mice. Come back to bed, darling," he patted the sheets and smiled. Looking at him now, I could tell his eyes weren't quite the right color. There was an unusual brightness to them. It occurred to me then that I was dreaming. It also occurred to me that the incubus was in my dream, pretending to be Alex.

"I'm going to have to ask you to leave."

He feigned looking hurt. "Oh, darling. Why? I've only just arrived. You DO want me, don't you?"

I shook my head. "I'm asking nicely. I know you aren't really who you seem to be. You aren't welcome here."

He sat up and slid across the bed toward me. "Darling, I think you're imagining things." He held out his arms. "Come, let me make it all better."

"No." I stepped back. "Really, you should go. I know dreams are your domain, but I'm a lucid dreamer. That puts me in control." Although I didn't always act on it, I frequently knew when I was in a dream, and knew how to shape the dream into whatever I wanted if I didn't care for the direction it was taking. Usually, I let it play out as it would, understanding that dreams serve as a problem-solving exercise for the brain.

His face twisted then and all semblance of Alex melted away. The incubus assumed his human form of Ian. "And just what do you think you can do to me, witch? Going to build a wall between us?"

"I could do," I said. "Or, I could just feed you to my cat."

He threw his head back and laughed, then fixed his gaze on me with a sneer. "I could crush your cat with one stamp of my foot."

I inclined my head toward the space behind him. "I'd like to see you try." A low growl drew his attention and he looked behind him. I'd envisioned Pip coming into the dream and growing to fill the entire space behind the incubus. Pip opened his maw and leaned toward the incubus, ready (and big enough) to nip his head right off. In a flash of light, the incubus disappeared. Pip's growling continued, and I awoke - really awoke - to find him on the pillow next to my head, growling and tapping a paw on my forehead in an attempt to rouse me.

I sat up and scooped him into my arms. "Thank you, my friend. That was a close thing." As I cuddled him, he quietened and began to purr softly. That was going to do it for me tonight as far as sleep went. I was shaking, and angry with myself for not thinking to ward my dreams. We knew the incubus couldn't enter dreams while on this plane, but now that he had returned to his own plane, any of us were fair game. It should have been obvious, warding against dream attacks, but I hadn't done it. Wards on the house and grounds protected from physical attack, and my fancy new personal protection ward worked for physical and psychic protection when I was conscious, but I'd neglected to consider psychic attacks to my unconscious mind.

"WHAT?!" Brighid was outraged when I called and told her later that morning. Luckily, I think she'd had time to get some coffee down her neck beforehand, since she then proceeded to merely gently berate me for neglecting to ward my dreams as opposed to screaming at me about it.

"Have you warded your own dreams?"

"Don't put this back on me, missy-thing," she said, then sighed. "No. But I will now. You've already done so, I presume?"

"Soon as I stopped shaking too much to light the candle. I've made a charm for Alex, too. Now that the incubus has been in my head, he knows what Alex looks like."

"Does this mean Ian knew how you feel about Alex?"

215

"I don't think so," I tucked the phone between my shoulder and ear while I opened the oven to remove the scones I'd baked for breakfast and adjusted the heat for cooking the turkey. "I think he might have just made the guess that we'd be attracted to each other after seeing us together at the bar and took a chance on it. The good news is that it didn't quite work out for him. The bad news is that he now knows for certain that I am attracted to Alex."

"Oh, sweetie!" I heard her slurp some more coffee. "I can't imagine what it was like. Are you OK? Such a violation!"

"Yeah. Well, I'm OK now, more or less. But I didn't sleep after that," I stifled another yawn, "so now I'm exhausted and it's only half past 8."

"What time is Alex coming?"

"I told him any time after 8:30, so he could arrive at any moment."

"You are going to tell him about it, aren't you?"

I sighed. "Yeah. At least, as much as I can get away with without completely embarrassing myself."

"I still think you should just tell him how you feel. I'm sure he feels the same. I have a sense for these sorts of things, you know."

I smiled. "Mmhmm. Well, it's complicated. What with all the time-travel rules and restrictions and all that."

"Oh, damn those rules and restrictions!"

"I completely agree, but that doesn't change anything." I pulled jam, butter and clotted cream from the fridge and set them on the counter. "I'm sure they're there for a very good reason."

"Says who?"

"Says the people who enacted them. They surely had the best of intentions."

"What are you going to do, Mora?"

"I don't know. I'm not sure there is anything to be done. There must be a reason the founders of the time travel thingy didn't want the demon hunters getting involved with the witches. Kind of like a no-fraternization policy on a job, I guess."

"Yeah, but people get around those all the time."

"I don't think there's a way of getting around this one, though." The coffee maker beeped and I grabbed a mug to pour myself a cup.

"Well, you definitely have to tell Alex about the dream - not least because Ian could use your attraction against you later, and you both need to be prepared for that." Brighid let out a frustrated groan. "Mom's bleating at me from the kitchen. I'd better go help. Good luck today, sweetie! Let me know how it goes!"

"I will! See you Saturday!" I put the phone back on the cradle and sipped my coffee. It was going to be a mild day, although it was starting out a bit overcast. It would warm up by lunchtime though, but the forecast was for some blustery winds to move in because of a late season tropical depression in the Atlantic, so I thought it would be nice to have our picnic in my private garden instead of on the beach as we'd originally planned.

We nibbled on scones and sipped coffee while we finished the lunch preparations. The small turkey breast was in the oven, and Alex was making his "famous cranberry relish", a recipe not known to him in his previous existence in Victorian England but now a favorite dish he had discovered while on a research mission several years ago. I organized the picnic hamper and told him about the incubus visiting my dreams pretending to be him. I sort of glossed over how I'd thought it really was him at first, and the excitement of believing that he really was as attracted to me as I was to him. In hindsight, it was obvious that it hadn't been the real Alex last night, but just in those first few moments…I blame it on having let my guard down in the relative peace we'd been enjoying these past several days.

"When I noticed him getting in bed, I put my hand out, you know, instinctively, sort of thing…" I paused to count the silverware. "And, when I touched his chest and didn't feel the triskele outline, I knew something wasn't right."

"He was counting on you believing it was me. He seems to assume we're more than just acquaintances," as he reached for his coffee mug, his hand brushed mine, sending a tingle up my arm.

"Aren't we?" I asked, and immediately regretted it. The words were out before I'd thought of what I was saying.

He turned to face me. "Well, yes, of course. I consider you a close friend." He turned back to his relish and I breathed a sigh, whether of relief or disappointment, I wasn't quite sure yet. I certainly was glad that my question hadn't come out as desperate sounding as I'd feared it might. "I know we've only known each other a relatively short time," he said, "but we have been through rather a lot."

I nodded. "I feel as if we've known each other for a lot longer than it's been. But, I wish we had more time. It seems like we went from meeting to becoming friendly to BAM! Sex! With not much getting-to-know-you in between!" We shared a laugh. "I know the sex was for the ritual, but still, I don't take it lightly. I...I wanted you to know that."

He reached over and took my hand in both of his. "I know. I don't either. It was," I watched as a bit of pink crept into his cheeks, "memorable. Whatever happens, no matter what the rest of my life brings me, I want you to know that I will treasure that memory - and our friendship - always."

Hmmm..."friendship". Was that truly the extent of his regard for me, or was it all he would admit to because we would soon be parted, presumably forever? "So, you've never tried to return to visit your other witch helpers?"

"No," he gave me a rueful smile, "rules and restrictions. That's the good and the bad of this vocation all rolled into one. Even before the leak and the demon hunting came into it, our society's members met with and got to know all kinds of people from all walks of life. Often you come to have a high regard for those you meet. And then, you have to leave, never to see them again."

I poured us both some more coffee. "Seems like a lonely existence."

"It can be I suppose. But, I knew that going into it. We have the company of other society members, of course. There aren't a lot of us, and we're close. As for anything besides friendships, other than the arranged engagement, I'd not had any serious relationships and was well on my way to a long naval career."

"Did you ever consider that you might meet someone in the course of the time travel work? Someone you might want to spend more time with?" I was cutting it close to an outright admission that I wanted to move our acquaintance to the next level. But, rather than being direct, I was going the roundabout way.

He fumbled the spoon and did a good job of catching it before it clattered onto the counter, slinging cranberry relish all over. "No. I…uh…no." Now he was fumbling his words. "Obviously, you have to…well, acknowledge the possibility, but it hadn't happened so far."

Hadn't, not hasn't. The tense of the word was not lost on me, and my heart beat a bit faster. But, then, he derailed the discussion.

"I think it's likely that the incubus was expecting you to fully believe I'd come to your bed last night. I suspect he would have been gone in the morning, and then when I showed up later and you asked where I'd gone - and I denied having been here - that it would have caused a proper row. I believe he was attempting to make me out to be a cad in order to throw you off balance, and gain an advantage."

Although I was annoyed at his change of subject, I had to admit his theory had merit. If I weren't a lucid dreamer, I might very well have been enchanted by the incubus to believe everything that happened in the dream was real. It was likely the demon wasn't fully aware of who Alex was, and what his role was in all this. But as it was hard to know how much Adaine might have told him, causing me any sort of emotional distress would affect the potency of my magic. Even with the advantage of complete trust in Alex - I would know he wasn't lying to me when he would have denied the visit - the stress of demon's deception and my believing it, however briefly, could have thrown me. On the one hand, it was flattering to think the demon considered me enough of a threat to attempt such a thing. On the other, given my already weakened state after the ritual - the specifics of which the demon also would not know about as I'd only discussed it with Brighid and Lingus, and Lingus had not shared the information with Adaine - the results could have been catastrophic.

"Here," Alex said, aiming a spoonful of the relish at my mouth, "taste."

"Mmmmmm, that's really very good!"

He smiled and went back to stirring. "I think we need to consider this the first volley of attack." He looked up at me. "I believe we may be seeing our demon sooner rather than later."

"Well, I suppose it's safe to assume that I've drawn its attention. Now I need to set the trap."

We had a lovely Thanksgiving picnic in the garden, but the conversation never again strayed close enough to personal feelings for me to nudge it without seeming like a lovelorn stalker. Brighid was not very happy with me about that, but was understanding.

"I know," she said over tea and biscuits Saturday afternoon. "It's hard enough to talk about feelings even when the other person isn't shutting you down."

"Well, really, he only did that once, and even then I'm sure it wasn't because he doesn't feel *something*. I think he's probably in the same frame of mind I'm in. We know that return visits are not allowed, so what would be the point in pursuing an impossible relationship?"

"Because, LOVE! Duh!"

"Oh, well that's that problem solved then." I made a face at her.

She sighed. "Sweetie, you know I only want you to be happy. But, I get it. I'm more of the 'better to have loved and lost' type, and you're more practical about it."

"You're more like the 'resistance is futile' type." I grabbed the dark chocolate Hob Nobs and shook more out onto the plate. Emotional eating, generally something to be avoided, but I wanted more Hob Nobs, dammit.

Brighid laughed and grabbed a cookie. "Yeah, I am. But, before you decide to play the Bronte tragic heroine, think it through. We don't know how much time you've got left, and I think you should make the most of it."

"Will you be here to help pick up the pieces of my shattered heart once he's left?" I darted a rueful glance at her.

She rolled her eyes at me. "Snark all you want but, yes. I WILL be here for you."

All day Saturday, with the exception of my *Messiah* rehearsal that morning, and our current tea break, Brighid and I had been making preparations to lay out the trap for the incubus. So when darkness fell, we were ready to do the work. Waiting until dark meant that all the other business in the area would be closed and there would be very few people about to wonder what we were up to. We had the advantage of a holiday weekend on our side, as well, meaning a lot of residents would be away visiting family, and off-season tourists should be few. We'd devised a two-fold trap, one that would prevent the incubus from getting too far away from us if - no, I shouldn't say if, I should say *when* - we managed to get the upper hand and he tried to escape. Originally, I'd thought my garden would be the place to center the trap, but then we thought it might be best to do it on the beach as there'd be plenty of room to work and good sight-lines to see who - or what - was coming at us. But with the storm churning off the coast, we worried the wind and sea swells might be too much, so we decided to go back to plan A and center the trap in the ritual circle of the main garden where the shop would help block some of the heavier winds and spray. It would mean undoing the protective wards on my property, but I would leave the wards on the building up, so we would have some means of respite, and a place to go for quick healings if needed. Getting in and out would be tricky as we fully expected to be harassed by as many lesser demons as the major demon could summon. Our two-fold trap still included the beach area, and should the demon not return until after the storm had passed, we could easily relocate the central trap back to the beach.

"The trick of it is for the demon not to know he's in the trap. It will make sense that I would want to shield myself and my friends with a protective circle, so he will expect this one," I pointed to the smaller circle on my diagram of the garden, "but not the hidden circle." I indicated the lightly outlined larger radius on the larger map encompassing all of my property, some of the wooded area beyond the shops, and the beach over the road.

"We can create some distractions for you around and between these points, so any lesser demons in the area will not know what you are doing." Eryn and Lingus had joined Brighid and me in my ritual room, and the Daemon queen studied my map for the waypoints I'd noted marking the larger circle's boundary. Alex was away, since he could not be privy to the planned trap.

"We feel fairly confident that the central trap will hold once he's in it," I caught Brighid's eye and she nodded in agreement, "but he will try to avoid crossing into it, I'm sure."

"Hopefully, he'll see something he can't resist," Brighid feigned a Mae West voice and twisted a ringlet around her finger while swaying her hips in her best va-va-voom stance. At my pointed glance, she gave me a sheepish smile and returned her attention to the map.

I glanced at the window and checked my watch. "I believe we're ready to start."

"I'll call our group," Eryn said, and she and Lingus drifted out of the window and into the night.

It happened two days later, when Alex, Brighid and I were eating pizza and preparing to binge-watch the latest series of *Doctor Who*. We were lucky to be all together when the tap on the window came and Lingus entered to tell us that Eryn's group had witnessed the demon re-entering our plane.

"We think he may be on his way here," Lingus turned to go back out to the garden, "you should prepare yourselves quickly."

"What? Now?" My heart skipped a beat. "He isn't going to take time to recover?"

"I gather he feels that he will be stronger than you, even in a weakened state." Lingus hovered just outside the window.

Brighid grabbed the bag with her tools from the three bags that we'd prepared for each of us and left by the door. One of Eryn's group would lead her to the place the demon would be most likely to enter. Once it was through, she would seal the outer circle, and the nature Daemons would reinforce that boundary. All of this was planned beforehand, and we'd been careful not to reveal any details of our work to Alex. If the incubus were to sense his consciousness, at least there would be no information of our plan to be gleaned from him. She gave me a fierce hug. "I'll be with you as soon as I can. Be careful!" She patted Alex on the arm and was out the door. Pip circled at my feet, agitated. He knew something was happening, and his hackles were up.

I looked at Alex. "It's too soon. I don't know if —"

Before the words were out, he closed the distance between us, took my face in his hands and lowered his head to meet my gaze. "You can do this. You've been preparing for weeks, you are nearly recovered from the ritual. You are ready - I know it." He lowered his hands to my shoulders. "Deep breath," I inhaled slowly and deeply. "Center yourself." As I released the breath, I envisioned all doubt and nervousness exiting with it. It sort of worked. At least, I felt my mind begin to focus on what was to come, and my instincts began to take over. Alex saw my resolve returning, and drew his hand across my cheek, smiling.

Out in the garden, Lingus and several Daemons were gathered waiting for us. A gust of wind whipped my hair as we moved to the ritual circle. I dropped my bag and pulled my hair back, twisting it into a knot at the base of my skull. "Is it getting windier? I thought the storm was still well off the coast and heading away from us."

Lingus raised his head and sniffed the air. "It is not. The storm is coming this way."

"How?" Alex moved to the far side of the circle and began setting out his tools.

Eryn appeared then, settling gently beside Lingus. "The incubus is drawing the storm to shore. And, it is growing stronger."

"He must think to use it against you, Morgaine," Lingus said.

"Dammit. As if things weren't bad enough, the bastard's bringing a bloody hurricane." I moved to the center of the circle and began the spell to prepare the trap. I was using a "trap-door" spell of my own devising, based on the information I'd found in the Ænigmata. Once the demon crossed the threshold, the circle would seal itself, trapping the incubus, and us, within. As I intoned the spell, the sigils I'd drawn around the perimeter began to glow. The fine hairs on my exposed skin tickled, as if reacting to a static charge, and a sudden rush of power around the circle sent a frisson through me. I turned to Alex where he knelt behind me, his tools arrayed before him. Our eyes met and he nodded, acknowledging his readiness. I took another deep breath and extended my arms toward him. Exhaling, I banished all negative thoughts, concentrating on freeing my mind of fear and doubt. Inhaling again, I visualized my toes as roots, snaking down into the ground, connecting with the earth and drawing upon its strength as a sapling draws nourishment from the soil.

I began working the spell of a misdirection field around Alex. He had explained that he needed to be as close to the incubus as he could be, but hidden if possible. "My working will allow me to open a portal, using the fetish, to banish the incubus. I need to be close when the portal opens so that it will draw the incubus in. But, the element of surprise can not be underestimated. If there is a way to hide me in plain sight…" And so we'd decided on the misdirection field. Hiding him from the demon while he began his working would be crucial. I hoped Brighid would be able to make it back in time. She would help strengthen the misdirection, giving Alex as much time as possible while I lured the demon in. It was a draining spell. Even were I at my full strength, I would hesitate to use it without Brighid's back-up. We could only hope the two of us would be strong enough, for long enough.

The words of the spell left my lips in a whisper accompanied by a soft, echoing murmur, but took physical shape as they floated on the air, a glowing mist that grew as the words flowed from me, encircling Alex. Once the spell finished, the mist shimmered and faded, shrinking to cocoon him and his tools like a cloak, reflecting the surrounding vegetation as if Alex were not there.

The wind was stronger still, whipping my skirt around my legs as I turned back to face toward the garden gate. Carefully, I released the wards on the property, but strengthened them on the building. Brighid ran through the gate and came to stand beside me. She was winded, having run all the way back using our prearranged shortcut. The demon would not be far behind.

"He's through," she said quietly, aware that Alex was close by and would not want to overhear. "Several lesser demons made it through before I finished sealing the circle, but Eryn's folk are enforcing the boundary now, so no others should be able to get through." Our outer circle would serve not only to keep the incubus close if he did not enter my trap here or if he somehow escaped it, but also as a protective barrier to keep more lesser demons out. With the strength and presence of the major demon, it was likely that any remaining effect from our bouquets would be greatly diminished.

The wind gusted even stronger, and stinging pellets of salted rain began falling. I found Brighid's hand and squeezed it. "Good luck, and be careful."

"You too," she said. She let go of my hand and softly began muttering spells to reinforce our protections, and the misdirection field hiding Alex.

I looked through the gate out toward the beach. I could clearly see the storm front approaching. As it moved onto the beach, it paused, slate colored clouds roiling and churning. Fingers of lightening streaked out, limning the underside of the clouds a blue-white glow. Slowly, the storm began moving toward us. As I lowered my eyes, the incubus in his human form of "Ian", strolled through my garden gate. It was as if he were dragging the storm along in his wake. I cast my eyes upward again as the storm clouds stretched out above us, covering the entire block and obscuring the last of the day's fading light. The wind turned colder, rain pelting us harder in the turmoil. Already we were soaking wet. "Ian" however seemed to stand in a bubble of calm, not a hair out of place.

"Greetings, witch," his voice was even, seductive. "Fine weather for it, mmm? I wonder: why is it you seem intent on meddling in my business?" His lips shaped a prim moue.

"Because you don't belong on this plane." My voice was strong, steady, but my heart was thundering.

The incubus laughed. "Oh, but I think I do. I quite like it here. So many lovely ladies. So much *mischief* to be made!" The corners of his mouth stretched upward in a gleeful smirk.

Brighid inhaled a shaky breath before continuing to murmur spells. This drew the incubus' attention. He smiled slyly. "Oh, I know you! Brighid, isn't it? I wondered where you'd got off to. Soooooo...you're a witch, too? How delicious!

I thought there was something unusual about your scent. Alas, I wasn't quite myself that night and didn't realize I'd nearly bedded a witch." His eyes drifted from her to me and back again. He held out a hand to her, and his eyes flashed. "Come, Brighid. Stand with me." He waved his other hand, and the bubble of calm expanded to include us. I could still feel the wind whipping just behind us.

I cut my eyes to Brighid. She hadn't reacted to the incubus. She stood defiantly, eyes averted, continuing her spellwork. Behind me, I could just make out Alex's murmured working, and hoped the wind between us would carry any sound of his utterances away from the incubus.

"Come, I said." The incubus was not expecting to be defied. Brighid had told me she had taken precautions in the event something like this happened. I was impressed. Whatever spell or ward she'd employed seemed to be working. I hadn't even considered that the incubus might try something like that on me. Luckily, he seemed to consider me either already immune to his charms, or not worth the bother. The incubus sneered at us. "No matter. I will waste you both. And your little pets," he said, glancing around at the assembled nature Daemons. Lingus caught my eye with a nearly imperceptible shake of his head. He had reassured me that the incubus could do them no harm, much as they could not harm him directly. The incubus didn't seem to have noticed. "I have pets of my own," he said, holding up his hands and gesturing. The lesser demons accompanying him poured into the garden then, fireballs flying. There were dozens of them. Lingus and the other Daemons began deflecting the fireballs, the rain helping to douse many as they hit the ground around us. One of them fell right at the edge of the circle, briefly flaring against the protective field Brighid was conjuring.

The incubus chuckled. "Surely you don't expect that your puny protections will keep me out of your circle." Good, it was working. The incubus did not suspect that the protective field was more for show than actual protection. We were counting on him mistaking the circle for a simple protection casting, and not the trap that it was. "I could do away with you from here, with a thought and a wave of my little finger," he waggled it at us as he spoke and my heart skipped a beat, "but I like this corporeal shell." He held his hands before him and took a step closer. "I like being able to touch…that tactile sensation of human skin beneath my fingertips. I wonder what it will feel like, crushing your pretty little throats with hands that could just as easily caress them."

He paused, just at the edge of the circle. The sigils on either side of the entryway glowed slightly brighter, reacting to his proximity. His brow furrowed and he peered around. "Where's your boyfriend? He's nearby," he said, nostrils flaring. "I can smell him." He thrust his hand out then, upright and fingers curled, as if he would claw the air. I flinched as he tilted his head to the side and rotated his hand as if to open a door, flinging his arm to the side. "A ha!" The incubus smiled triumphantly and sniffed the air again. "Not another witch, at least. You thought you could hide him, spring some sort of surprise fisticuffs on me?" He laughed.

I peered over my shoulder. I already knew the misdirection field was gone, I'd felt it as the incubus tore it away. Alex had moved closer to me and was standing tall, in a fencing stance. One hand, likely holding the fetish, was behind his back, his other holding his athame at the ready. He was keeping his mouth steady, but I could tell he was uttering words behind his clenched teeth. Even exposed, he was still working his banishment. But, for all the incubus could tell, Alex could have been praying.

The incubus heaved a sigh and shook his head. "Such bravery. That's what I like about you humans. Always *hoping* - even in the face of certain defeat." He lifted his foot and began to step over the threshold. The sigils burned even brighter. There came a shrill warning cry from one of the lesser demons who, noticing the sigils, had paused its attack on us to sound an alert. The incubus looked down, and stepped back. When he looked back at me, his face was twisted in fury. "You clever, clever girl. You tried to spring a trap on me."

The misdirection field gone, Brighid had shifted all of her spellworking to keeping our personal protection fields strengthened. If she shared the terror I was beginning to feel, that he could reach through our protection fields as easily as he tore away Alex's misdirection field, she showed no sign of it, concentrating on uttering the words of the spell. I took solace in her strength and cleared my mind, ready to do whatever I had to do to protect us all.

Drawing on notes I'd made from the Ænigmata, I began forming a spell, one I hoped would paralyze the incubus long enough for Alex to finish his working and open the portal to banish the fiend. This was dark working, and I was putting my very soul at risk attempting it.

"Oh, no you don't!" The incubus was too fast for me, and before I could finish my incantation, he thrust both arms at us. A gust of heated air exploded in front of us and sent the three of us sprawling backward. I heard a sickening crack and felt the jarring of my head banging against a stone bench at the perimeter of the ritual space as I slid backward into it. A bright flash of light and audible 'pop' confirmed that our entrapment circle was broken. My vision swam as I struggled to sit up, to see if Alex and Brighid were hurt.

The incubus advanced across the broken circle, scattering herbs and candles, and loomed over me. He smiled, but it was a horrid, vicious display of sharpened teeth, droplets of blood forming from cuts the teeth made to his lips and mouth. His human glamour was starting to fade. "You want to play, do you? I've got all of eternity on this plane. I've a mind to let you live for a while, knowing that I can rip you from existence at any moment - let you marinate in fear before I feed you to the Darkness."

As my vision started to fade, I saw the incubus turn and storm away. He paused before reaching the gate, gestured over his head, and stalked out into the night. The storm he released grew around us again, intensifying. The last thing I heard before passing out was Alex calling my name.

Chapter Thirteen

struggled to open my eyes. Not knowing where I was at first was all the more disconcerting given the storm now raging around us. Finally, I forced my eyes open and found myself staring at Alex's upside down face. He was on his knees behind me, my head on his lap. To his right, Brighid leaned in, pushing a loosened strand of hair away from my eyes. Lingus and Eryn were on Alex's left. Memory rushed back, and I knew where I was and what had happened. I struggled to sit up, but Alex put his hands on my shoulders and held me down.

"Easy," he said. "You've taken quite a hit to the bonce."

"Bonce?" Brighid said.

"Bonce," said Alex, "head, noggin, pate."

I groaned. "How long was I out? What happened to the incubus? Are all of you all right?"

"Slow down!" Brighid shook her head at me. "You've been out a couple of minutes - three, tops. We're all OK."

"The incubus is on the beach," Eryn said. "He has discovered that he is trapped after all."

"Lemme up!"

"Slowly!" Alex admonished, supporting my neck and shoulders as I sat. I took a moment to allow the dizziness to pass.

"Lingus, Eryn, and I have done a quick healing on you," Brighid said. "You cracked your head but good when the bastard blasted us. There doesn't appear to be a fracture, and we've stopped the bleeding, but you're going to have one hell of a headache later."

"Thank you," I said meeting each of their gazes. "I think I can stand now. I want to finish this before he can rally."

Lingus placed a hand on my arm. "Morgaine, that spell you were attempting - I do not think you should use it. It is too risky."

I shook my head. "It's all I've got left! I don't know of any other way of stopping him long enough to give Alex the time he needs to open the portal. If I'd got him in the circle, we'd be cracking open a bottle of champagne and celebrating, but he didn't fall for it, and the larger circle is too big for Alex's working to have an effect. He has to be close to the bastard."

"There may be another way," Lingus said. "As nature Daemons, we have some control over storms. And, I believe witches can use that energy as well."

"Goddess preserve us! Why didn't we think of that?!" Brighid lightly punched my arm.

"Well, it did occur to me briefly," I admitted, "but you know what I'm like with storm energy."

Alex looked confused. "Storm energy?"

"Here, help me stand," I reached out for his hand and he pulled me to my feet. "Do you know how people are always yelling at the meteorologists whenever a forecast doesn't work out as planned? A storm turns out either more or less intense than predicted, or doesn't materialize at all?" Alex nodded. "Well, witches can draw energy from the weather for ritual or spell work."

"Ah," Alex said, a smile spreading across his face. "I think I get it. The weather prognosticators - you quite literally," he waggled his eyebrows, "steal their thunder!"

"Yes!" I said, returning his smile. "'Steal their thunder'. Very clever." I looked around and took in the smiles of amusement on the faces of my friends. It made me almost feel that maybe all was not lost after all. I addressed Lingus and Eryn. "How can we use this storm, then? As I said, weather magic has never been my strong suit. Whenever I've tried to use it, things never work out the way I want them to. I've never been able to direct the energy to do my bidding. Besides, drawing energy from it for spellwork is one thing. I don't think the amount of energy we are able to draw will be enough to fight an incubus."

Eryn gestured and the five of us began walking toward the gate. When we reached the back of the building, our feet sloshed in several inches of water. A storm surge was flooding inland. Somehow, Eryn's voice carried to us over the din of the storm. "We will work to channel the power of the storm into you, Morgaine. Not just draw from it, but draw *it* into you, if you understand." I wasn't sure I did, but I nodded anyway. "You should be able to use it to build a trap of natural origins for the incubus. It sounds as if perhaps in the past you have been fighting the energy instead of working within its bounds." She paused at the gate and looked back at me. "I wish to reaffirm what Lingus has said. That spell you were attempting earlier should be the absolute last resort. It is unpredictable, and we would not be able to fix the consequences as easily as we healed your head if something with that spell were to go awry."

I nodded and we stepped out into the full force of the storm. Wind, rain, and sea spray battered us as we tried to make out the scene on the beach. The incubus was there, railing against the secondary trap. Flashes of light bounced harmlessly off the invisible dome of the trap as he threw bolts of energy at it.

"The boundary holds," Eryn said.

"Where are the lesser demons?" Brighid asked. "They don't seem to be helping him."

One of Eryn's group murmured something to her and she turned to us. "Once they realized they were trapped as well, the incubus' hold over them appeared to have broken down. They are trying to save themselves it seems, and are no longer interested in the incubus' fight with you."

"Well that's some small comfort," I said. "At least maybe we won't be fighting them off as well."

"Are you ready, Morgaine? Alex?" Lingus was peering into the storm above us.

Alex and I exchanged a glance and nodded. The storm surge was receding, leaving soaked sand in its wake, but the roadway and the shops across from the beach, including my own, would have standing water for some time yet.

Eryn led us across the street, and we strained against the wind to remain upright as we crossed to the edge of the beach. "Brighid, we can use your help channeling the storm. We will remain behind Morgaine and Alex. If the incubus senses what we are doing, he may attack us - and if any of his lesser demon friends are inclined to help, we will have that to deal with as well. I will call my guard to help defend us." Eryn looked at me then. "Morgaine, try to keep the protective wards strong around you and Alex while we channel the storm's energy. Until you feel the power of the storm moving

within you, the two of you will be vulnerable to the incubus."
I nodded.

"Let us begin," Lingus said.

Alex and I stepped toward the incubus with Brighid,
Eryn, Lingus, and several of Eryn's group following closely
behind. I could hear Eryn murmuring further instructions to
Brighid as we progressed. We stopped about 100 feet away
from the incubus. More of his human glamour had faded and
he now moved in an animalistic way, pacing near the
boundary, growling and flinging his energy bolts at it. Just the
knowledge that we'd managed to trap him after all seemed to
put him off balance, and he took no notice of us as we
approached. A rhythmic murmuring began behind us, our
friends had begun their spell to channel the storm's power to
me. Balancing my thoughts despite the pounding in my head,
I poured half of my attention into reinforcing Alex's and my
protective wards, the other half into opening myself up to the
power of the storm. Alex, having made use of his pockets and
waistband to carry his other tools with him, began placing the
other fetishes in the sand around us.

Shortly after we started our incantations again, the
incubus noticed us. He advanced toward us, but stopped a
few feet away, drawing ragged breaths, the wind and water
tearing at him now as well as us. "I underestimated you,
witch." He stood tall and some of the wildness fell away as he
pulled a bit of his human glamour back into place. "Do not
mistake that for weakness on my part, however." He cast a
glance around at the boundary. "If I were the deal-making
sort, I'd offer to not kill you immediately if you release this
boundary. Very generous of me, that would be, and I was

quite looking forward to toying with you for a while. You have proven to be rather formidable. I like a challenge."

My heart pounded in my chest. Behind me, the group continued murmuring their spell. Beside me, Alex whispered his own incantation. Both hands were behind his back, clutching the fetish.

"Oh, but you see," the incubus turned his attention back to me. "I grow weary of this. I can smell you all over this working," he gestured to the boundary. "When you are dead, the trap will fail."

Behind me, the whispered incantation of Eryn, Lingus, and Brighid took on a frenetic note. Especially in Brighid's voice, I could sense a bit of panic. It didn't seem to be working, I wasn't feeling anything. I murmured my own incantation, one I'd used before when trying to use storm magic. Nothing. The incubus paced toward me, and I instinctively raised my arms and I sent out a blocking ward. He stopped, but sneered. "You surely don't expect that to keep me out. I thought I proved most effectively that your power is no match for mine." He favored me with a mock look of concern. "How's your head?"

I altered my incantation, trying to coax the storm to lend me it's energy, but that didn't work either. Just as I thought I was going to have to try the Ænigmata spell again, I heard Lingus over the noise of the storm.

"Don't try to take the energy, Morgaine, just *accept* it!" I puzzled over his meaning, panic rising as the incubus drew his hands together and began to build his offense. *Accept it, accept it…what does that mean?!"* I tried to concentrate on my core, willing myself to relax, and to open, releasing my instinctive guards against outside forces. That worked! Finally I felt the power of the storm entering me. My blood sang with the strength of the natural elements, my skin tingled as a pocket of calm seemed to form around me and Alex, a barrier blending with my blocking ward, obstructing the brunt of the storm's force, as if I had become the storm's eye. I tried to direct the energy, wishing for a gust of wind to push the incubus to the ground and hold him there, but it wouldn't come. I struggled to push the wind at him. Panic again threatened to overcome me. *This was what I was trying to tell them - I can't control it!* The demon, head tilted down, concentrating on his own building magic, lifted his eyes to me and smiled, as if he could sense my frantic struggle to wield a defense.

Then, Eryn's voice was close in my ear, either she had moved closer, or was somehow directing her voice to me. I heard her words clearly, "Don't try to control the power, Morgaine, *feel* it. Let it guide you. *Be* the storm, don't just try to brandish it. Let it work through you."

Despite the rush of anxiety, I forced my mind to be still. I relaxed my muscles, and dropped my concentration on our protection wards, focusing solely on receiving the storm's power and letting it take me over. Things seemed to move in slow-motion then and I was aware of everything happening around me. The incubus was drawing back his arms to launch its attack, Alex was intoning his banishment spell, the fetish clasped in his hands beginning to glow in my periphery vision. The other statuettes Alex had placed around us also began to glow, but the incubus was taking no notice. A few of the lesser demons gathering to join the incubus against us once more. Brighid and our Daemon friends approaching to form a semi-circle around us, bracing to deflect anything the incubus succeeded in throwing at us.

I raised my arms to the storm above and fully welcomed it into me. A crackle of electricity zinged through me and I began speaking then, a language I was not aware I knew, and probably would not remember after this night. As with the misdirection field spell, the words manifested as a mist as they left my mouth, thickening into a dense fog.

"What are you doing?" The incubus stared around at all of us, noticing then that something extraordinary was happening. He'd been focusing his ire solely on me since we'd approached, and only now considered that I was not the only threat to him. He lobbed a glowing ball of energy toward us, so filled with malevolence that it spit and crackled viciously. The Daemons and Brighid had managed a strong barrier between us and the incubus, but it didn't hold completely. Cracks appeared and shattered sparks pushed through as the barrier splintered, striking us and sizzling as they burned skin or clothing. Ignoring the pain, I continued intoning the storm's spell. Alex flinched, but carried on too, the fetish growing brighter and brighter. He brought his hands around to hold it before him as he continued working his spell. The lesser demons, their own fireballs having been no match for our protective barrier, scattered at the sight of the glowing fetish.

"Nooooooo!" The incubus howled, recognizing the portal forming. He aimed his strikes fully at Alex and the fetish, and I nearly lost the communion with the storm when the barrier shattered and I heard Alex cry out as he was showered with sparks. I quickly uttered a healing spell while Brighid and the Daemons directed their energies at rebuilding and reinforcing the protective barrier around us. Alex stood strong, despite the obvious pain from the incubus' attacks.

The storm's energy coiled within me, ready to strike at my will. Understanding now that I only needed to allow the energy to know my wishes, and not try to direct it to do my bidding, I envisioned it strengthening the barrier. I felt a tingling sensation, and the barrier began to glow slightly. The next attack by the demon resulted in his energy bolt disintegrating to ash as it struck the barrier, falling harmlessly to the ground.

Now it was the incubus' turn to panic, and it began to back away, still slinging the bolts, trying to strengthen them, to no avail. He began to look around wildly for escape, calling the lesser demons to him, without success. All the while, the fog I was making circled around him, thicker and faster, spinning into a funnel concentrated at his feet. He looked down as the funnel began growing and moving up his calves. "No. No!" He tried to jump over the funnel, but it tripped him up and he stumbled, regaining his feet unsteadily as higher and higher the funnel rose, a compact, concentrated vortex, pinning the incubus to the spot.

Alex's voice rose, the words of his spell spilling into the air over the noise of the storm. The fetish grew brighter, blue-white light stretching into a golden glow as fingers of energy reached out toward the incubus. Alex knelt and placed the fetish in the sand between himself and the incubus.

The incubus was in a full panic now, screaming and struggling against the vortex. Casting about himself, he used his power to draw as many of the nearby lesser demons to him as he could. Grabbing them, he opened his mouth wide, wider than should be possible. Unhinging his jaw, he devoured as many of the demons as he could reach, one by one.

"He's trying to absorb their energy," I heard Lingus shout.

The incubus fixed me with his vicious gaze. He spoke a few words in a language I'd never heard before and I felt a tugging sensation at my core. Confused, my concentration faltered, panic threatening to overcome me. But I would not let that happen. I focused my attention on the tugging sensation, and understood what was happening. The incubus was attempting to pull the storm away from me, to regain control over it. I heard voices rise behind me, my friends redoubling their efforts to help me hang on to the storm's energy. Then, the tugging sensation subsided as I felt the energy of the storm itself repelling pull of the incubus.

Realizing the storm energy would not obey, the incubus drew itself up and shifted all of its energy and that stolen from the lesser demons into fashioning a huge ball of furious malevolence. It spat green, black, and white sparks. The demon's own skin was being seared by this enormous, deadly orb. All the while, the portal Alex summoned grew larger, it's reaching fingers stretching closer and closer to the incubus. As they tickled the outside of the vortex, wisps of the fog reached back toward the fetish's fingers of energy, then an opening appeared providing access to the incubus. The incubus took advantage of that opening to free himself partially, rearing back to heave the orb at us.

"Oh, shit," I heard Brighid say. She realized, as I did in that moment, that our barrier would not withstand this final attack. I struggled to keep my panic in check, and trusted in the storm's energy.

As the portal's energy strands snaked through the opening in my vortex, two separate fingers of energy emerged from it, one making it's way from the fetish to Alex, the other to me, then another beam of energy formed between the two of us, forming a triangle with the fetish at the top and Alex and I at the base. When the circuit closed, I felt a burst of energy as it combined it's power with that of the storm's energy. Having been part of the creation of the fetish, I was now the recipient of it's powers along with Alex. The vortex strengthened and tightened, restricting the incubus' movement once again. He howled once more, and loosed the orb toward us. It fell short and lay on the sand, sputtering and writhing like a living thing. The portal's energy strands moved through the vortex as if a part of it, winding themselves around the incubus, coil after coil like a rope until the incubus was completely enclosed. I released the vortex as the portal grew brighter, the glow from the strands around the incubus obscuring him completely from our view. With a whooping sound and a blast of hot wind, the portal snapped shut, taking the incubus with it. The orb left by the incubus collapsed in on itself until it winked out of existence. The glowing of the fetish faded until it was once more a just a wooden carving, though little puffs of steam arose from it where droplets of rain and sea water struck it.

I stared at it, the storm's power still coursing through me, until I felt Eryn's gentle touch. "Release the storm, Morgaine. You have done well."

I inhaled deeply, and as I exhaled, the storm's energy faded from me. Suddenly, I had no strength. Head swimming, I felt my knees buckling, and Alex rushed forward to catch me before I crashed to the ground. Instead, we both sank gently to the wet sand, and watched as the nature Daemons coaxed the storm back out to sea.

"**C**old. So-o-o-o co-o-o-ld," I muttered through chattering teeth. Soaked to the bone, shivering violently, and head pounding, I felt consciousness leaving me once again.

Eryn felt my forehead. "We must get her inside and warmed up. Quickly now."

Alex scooped me up into his arms, and rushed back to the shop, Brighid, Eryn, and Lingus in his wake. Though wind was subsiding, gusts still bandied about us, and every breath of breeze on my skin set me shivering even more. I faded out, and the next awareness was of Alex holding me up while Brighid peeled off my sodden clothes. I could hear the shower running, and felt the warmth of the steam. I don't remember much of the shower itself, except coming to and having Brighid tease me.

"You really need a tub for things like this, so it will be easier to warm you up next time you decide to help vanquish a demon in the midst of a category one hurricane in December." She and Alex, stripped to their underwear, held me under the hot water until my teeth stopped chattering.

Next, I came to wrapped in towels from head to toe, sitting on the bed leaning against Alex.

"Brighid, how are you holding up," he asked. "Is there anything I can do for you?"

"No, I'll be fine," she said. She was wrapped in one of my robes, toweling her hair dry. "I think we could all use a cup of tea." She tossed the towel in the hamper. "Be right back."

Later, after having been roused enough to sip the hot tea while propped against Alex as he sat on the bed behind me, I slipped into a fitful doze. Alex got into bed under the covers with me, and held me while I drifted in and out of sleep. I have vague remembrances of waking, shivering, but feeling his warmth surrounding me, and hearing him utter soothing words until I drifted off again.

Next morning, I awoke with a start to find myself alone. I panicked, worried that Alex had been made to leave after the demon was gone and that I'd not had a chance to say goodbye. "Alex?!" I called. "Brighid?! Anyone?" Pip pushed through the opening of the cracked doorway and leapt up onto the bed, purring and head-butting me, followed closely by Alex.

"I'm here," he said, smiling and sitting on the side of the bed. "How are you feeling? Brighid's getting you some coffee."

"OK, I think. Head's a bit achy, though." My heart had been pounding when I awoke alone, and now that Alex was sitting in front of me, I could feel myself calming. I could not imagine what I would have done if I'd missed seeing him again before he had to leave.

"I'm not surprised," Brighid came in and handed me the steaming cup of coffee. "You're lucky all you have is a headache. Between getting blasted into the bench, and then getting possessed by a raging storm, it's a wonder you're even sitting up!"

"Are you guys all right?" I said. "And the Daemons?"

"We're all fine," she smiled and pulled me into a hug. Then she started bouncing, while still holding me, causing me to nearly sling the coffee all over my bedclothes. "You did it!!"

"WE did it," I corrected, as Alex rescued my coffee before it spilled. "By the way, how did you manage to resist the incubus calling to you early on? He seemed so sure you would just rush to his side when he told you to."

"Oh, that!" She reached over to the nightstand and palmed something. An impish smile played at her lips as she opened her hand to reveal two small pink cone shapes. "Earplugs!" she laughed. "And, I unfocused my eyes to keep him from tempting me with his hot human form!"

Alex grinned and nodded approvingly.

"You clever girl!" I said. "Without you, I don't think I could have finished that battle. Whatever magic you worked with Eryn and Lingus on that storm made it possible. And of course, Alex's banishing spell was rather a big part of it."

Alex smiled and handed me back the coffee as Brighid stopped bouncing and let me go. "It was certainly a team effort, but you did an amazing job wielding the power of the storm, Morgaine."

"I'm so glad Lingus thought of it, instead of me using that spell," I gave an involuntary shudder at the memory.

"Yes," said Alex. "He's quite cunning, Lingus"

Brighid and I looked at each other, eyes wide, and burst out laughing at the near homophone he had unwittingly made.

Alex's brow furrowed. "What?" He looked at each of us in turn. "What's so fun— Oh!" he said, as the realization hit. "You two are like a gaggle of teenage boys!" he said, reprovingly, but smiled anyway.

"Speaking of the storm, I bet my shop is flooded." Alex and Brighid shared a glance and their smiles faded. "What?" I said. "Tell…"

"A bit more than just flooded, I'm afraid," Alex gave me a pained look. "The main windows were broken out, and the wind and rain took quite a bit of a toll on your inventory. I've boarded the windows over for now, and Brighid and I have cleaned up some."

I sighed. "Thank you both. And, thank the Goddess for good insurance. What about the rest of the street - or the village, for that matter?"

"Most of the shops have some level of destruction," Brighid said. "I think your shop took the brunt of it since the storm was pretty much directly over or around it. The village has some typical wind and flood damage associated with strong tropical storms, but no injuries or major flooding or service outages, thankfully."

"It's all over the news about the odd storm," Alex smiled. "The weathermen and women are scrambling to explain how a diminishing tropical storm off the coast managed to make a sharp left, intensify briefly into a category one hurricane - albeit a very compact one, seemingly centered just over a portion of the village - and then drift harmlessly back to sea a couple of hours later."

"Well," I said, "no doubt Celia Davidson will blame me for this too - only this time, she'll be right!"

 spent the whole of that day mostly in bed with my friends around me. Alex promised he wouldn't go before saying goodbye, so I was able to have a righteous nap

that afternoon, and woke up feeling refreshed around dinner time. We got pizza, and binge-watched *Doctor Who*, making up for our interrupted pizza party the night before.

The next day, we went out to help with the clean up around the village. There was less to do than I'd expected, and most damage had already been dealt with. Our street was the hardest hit, but luckily no one had any severe damage. Brighid was right, my shop seemed to have experienced the brunt of the storm. I called my insurance company, and made arrangements to have the broken windows replaced. Alex and Brighid helped me with an inventory of damaged stock to submit to the insurance adjuster. It seemed such a normal thing to be doing, sorting things out after a storm. There were moments when I almost forgot the cause and origin of the storm. But when I'd catch Alex's eye, and saw the look of pride he gave me, the events of that night flashed again in my mind. It's normal to feel pride in a job well done, but mostly, I just felt lucky.

When I came home from the Saturday's rehearsal of *The Messiah*, Alex was setting the table, a roasted chicken was resting on the counter top and the aroma of Yorkshire Puddings filled the air. Brighid was nowhere to be seen and Lingus and Eryn had not been heard from since Thursday, although they assured me they were never far away and would come if we needed them.

"Mmmm...it smells divine in here!" I tossed my purse onto a nearby chair and walked to the kitchen to peek under the foil tent at the chicken.

"Ah-ah-ah," Alex said, playfully swiping at my hand. "It's still resting."

I looked around at the rest of the dishes - roasted potatoes and parsnips, green beans, gravy bubbling gently on the stove. "You're making a proper roast dinner!"

"I am," Alex flashed me a beatific smile. "It's been a while since I've had one, and I thought we both deserved a treat after recent events." There was something up, though. Something about the timbre of his voice, pitched down despite his jovial words.

I stared at his back as he poured us both a glass of wine. It was my favorite, Sebastiani Cabernet. My heart sank. "You're leaving, aren't you?"

He paused, bottle hovering over one of the glasses before he carefully set it down and turned to face me. "I've been called back. There are signs that another demon has breached the planal barrier and I'll be sent to deal with it."

Knowing that this day would come did not make it any easier to accept. I wasn't ready yet. "I thought maybe you'd have a bit of a reprieve," I said, distancing myself from my own feelings. "You know, bit of a break, hang out with friends, relax…"

He nodded. "It's been a few days. I'm lucky I haven't been called back sooner, really. It's just…there aren't that many of us, and it's all hands on deck…" He gave me a smile. "Anyway, that's why I've taken over your kitchen for this meal. We both like a good roast dinner, and I don't know when I'll get another, so…"

"If there were some way for you to visit, you could come for dinner anytime you liked." I didn't try to hide my disappointment.

"I know, I wish there was a way. But, let's not be sad. I've made us this fabulous dinner, and damn it, we deserve to enjoy it." He picked up the wine glasses and handed one to me. "A toast," he said, catching and holding my gaze. "To good friends - no matter how short the time together," he paused, eyes locked on mine, "they are always in our hearts." I did not miss the subtext. It was hard not to toss the wine away and pull him into a kiss, to tell him how I felt. But, the knowledge that we would soon be parted indefinitely (I still refused to accept that it would be forever), tempered my instincts. Instead, I forced a smile.

"Good friends," I said, and we clinked glasses. "Oh, and to helpful Daemons." *clink*

"To cooperative storms," he added. *clink* Now we were just getting silly.

"To demon snatching portals!" *clink*

Alex laughed. "To…to…"

"To not burning the Yorkshires!" Alex's eyes flew wide as I grabbed the oven mitt and scooted around him to open the oven. A puff of bluish smoke belched out and I waved vigorously to disperse it. I pulled the Yorkshire Puddings out of the oven and placed them on a potholder. They were a little browner than was necessary, but not yet burnt.

"Good save!" he said. We laughed then, and I relaxed a bit. I was determined not to be morose in the time we had left.

It was a good dinner, and after we tidied the kitchen, we relaxed on the sofa and finished the bottle of wine between us. Pip claimed Alex's lap and seemed determined to not let him get up.

"You're going to break my kitty's heart when you leave, you know." *And mine, too.*

Alex chuckled and scratched Pip behind the ears. Pip responded by purring even louder. "I'm going to miss this little fuzz ball. He is one intelligent creature, your Pip."

"I know. I'm grateful that he adopted me." We both laughed, and Pip stretched, taking up even more real estate on Alex's lap.

Alex took my hand and we sat in silence for a few minutes. Again, I was struggling with whether to tell him of my feelings or not. I suspected he knew, and I also suspected he returned those feelings. And, I felt fairly confident he was struggling with the same turmoil as I. We were going to be miserable apart, but would we be even more miserable for having voiced our feelings knowing that there was nothing we could do about them?

"I've put this off longer than I should have," he said. "It's time."

Pip growled when Alex stood and gently settled him onto the sofa. I didn't blame him. I stood too and Alex pulled me into his arms. I rested my head on his chest and his chin settled on top of my head as he curled into me. I felt Pip brushing against our legs, figure eights between the two of us. A prickle of tears stung my eyes as we parted. Alex's eyes shone, too, but both of us managed to keep the tears in check.

Kneeling, Alex petted Pip. "Look after your mistress for me, Pip." Pip mewled in acknowledgment, but let out a mournful yowl as Alex stood again. He sat on his haunches between us, wrapping his tail around him, and looked up at us.

"We're going to miss you," I said. "Please promise me you'll try to come visit. Pester them, tell them that rule is ridiculous!"

He smiled, "I will try, I promise. If there is a way, I'll bloody well find it!"

"Please, be careful."

"I will," Alex said. "Take care, my brave witch." He cupped my face with one hand and laid the other across his heart, bowing slightly, his eyes never leaving mine. And then, he was gone.

 must have stood there, staring into the space he'd occupied, for ten minutes or more, my hand against my cheek, where his had been. Finally, I curled up on the sofa with Pip. I would be lying if I said I didn't cry. Not only did I cry, it was what we call the ugly cry. Sobbing so violently it was hard to catch my breath, red-faced, tears and snot making rivers through my makeup. Pip yowled right along with me, as if distressed not only that his friend had left, but that he couldn't do anything to make me feel better.

I almost didn't answer when the phone rang, but I knew it was Brighid, and I knew why she was calling.

She didn't even let me say "hello" first. "He's gone, hasn't he? I felt you break."

"About an hour ago." My voice shuddered, even though the worst of the sobbing had subsided.

"I'm coming over."

"No. Please, I'd rather be alone tonight. Come tomorrow?"

"OK," she said, reluctantly. "But call me - no matter what time - if you need me before then. Promise."

"I will, I promise."

I eventually pulled myself together enough to put myself to bed, but I didn't sleep. The sobbing eased sometime in the early morning hours, but I remained teary. Pip did his best to comfort me, and we stayed snuggled in bed until the sun was up.

Brighid let herself in and crawled on the bed with us, scooping me and Pip up in a hug. "I'm so sorry, Mora."

I sniffled and sat up. "I knew it was coming, but I wasn't ready."

"Oh, sweetie. I don't think you were ever going to be ready."

She was right. "I didn't tell him, in the end," I said and waited for her reaction. Her face remained still, no trace of judgment, or disappointment. "I couldn't bring myself to do it. I might never see him again. How could I burden him with the absolute knowledge of my feelings knowing that we might never be able to see each other again? I just…couldn't tell him. I couldn't have him compromised in any future works he might have to do if he was thinking about me."

She pulled me into a hug again. "It's OK. I understand."

"I'm sure he feels something for me. I could tell, just looking in his eyes. But, he didn't say anything either."

"I really think you were right the other day. I think you're both trying to protect each other. If you don't say the words, then after a while, maybe you can pretend it isn't true. It's a coping mechanism. I get it."

Brighid stayed with me for the next several days, giving me space, but always present. She made sure I ate, despite my complete lack of appetite. Even Pip seemed to be off his food, but she managed to coax him to eat, as well. Sleep was ever elusive, and when it came it was filled with either nightmares of me searching for Alex and always just missing him, or replays of the night we vanquished the demon. I closed the shop until further notice. No one would question it, since I was still dealing with the storm damage. I didn't know when I'd re-open. I couldn't even think about it.

It was all I could do, just existing for the next couple of weeks. Rehearsals for *The Messiah* came and went, with me going through the motions. I chatted and interacted with my fellow choir members, and did my best to maintain a cheerful attitude. The night of the performance arrived, and happened to fall on Yuletide, the winter solstice. I sang well, but there was not the usual joy in it for me. Father Wil and his wife hosted an after-performance party, but I made an excuse of feeling a little under the weather and came home instead. I'd had enough pretending to be jovial by that point. It wasn't that I just wanted to come home and wallow. Well, OK, yes, it was. I admit, I was indulging myself with my misery. I knew I would get with it eventually, but I just wanted that one last pity session.

I let myself have a good cry, then took a shower and got ready for bed. Meditation is a wonderful way of getting your equilibrium back after a bad time, but I'd not done one since before Alex left. I did one this night, determined to have a good night's rest and to start pulling myself back together tomorrow. Laying on my back in the bed, Pip on the pillow next to my head, purring soothingly, I finally felt myself drifting off into a real sleep.

I was awakened several hours later, a strange pressure on my chest, strange visuals swirling through my head. I sat up with a start and felt something drop into my lap. I turned the lamp on and looked to see what it was. All I could see was a leather cord trailing from folds in the covers. I picked it up. As end of the cord cleared the folds, I saw a disc attached to it. It spun and caught the light. It was Alex's Tempus Purus amulet. I set the stone in my hand. As soon as the amulet touched my skin, my mind was bombarded by images, colors, flashing lights. I dropped the amulet back onto the covers and grabbed my head, trying to clear it.

"Too much," I said. "I can't…"

Pip was watching, a low growl emanating from his throat. I felt warmth and movement on my lap. It was the amulet. It was vibrating and emitting heat.

I stretched a finger toward it. "I…I don't know if you can hear me, or understand… I think you're trying to tell me something, but it's too much. I can't process all that information. Can you go more slowly?" I touched the surface. The images and impressions came again, still frantic, but it seemed as if the amulet was trying to make itself understood. I tried not to fight it, to let the impressions wash over me. I pushed my mind into a meditative state, and the images started to coalesce and make sense.

There was an image of me lying in the bed, shivering, strands of still-damp hair clinging to my face. I was seeing myself as Alex had the night of the storm. He climbed under the covers, pulling me into his arms, smoothing the hair from my face, murmuring assurances to me until I drifted off to sleep. Then there was an impression of us just before he left. And I could hear his thoughts.

"She is the most beautiful creature I have ever seen," he thought. *"I should take her in my arms, carry her to the bedroom and worship her like the goddess she is."*

In the vision, I was telling him to be careful, and to try to come back.

"I will never stop trying to come back. I love you." His thoughts were in my head as if they were my own. *"But, I can't tell you. It would be selfish of me. And cruel, to tell you how I feel and then leave you forever. How could I do that to you? You deserve so much more. You deserve all the happiness in the world."*

Tears were streaming down my cheeks. Pip was mewling pitifully, as if he had experienced all of that as well, and maybe he had. I didn't know how this amulet sentience thing worked, after all. The vision shifted again then. But it was harried and not very lucid. Alex was attempting to banish a demon, that much was clear, but something was going wrong. My vision swam red, reminding me of when I hit my head the night of the storm. Pain seared through my head. The vision cleared slightly, but was still blurry. I - or Alex, rather - was coming to in a dark place. Twisted creatures were moving around him. Occasionally one would lash at him, raking him with sharp talons, or throwing hot coals at him, singeing his clothes and skin. I panicked then. Something was wrong. Something was very, very wrong.

I dropped the amulet and leapt out of bed, grabbing for my clothes. I had to call Brighid. I would find Alex, somehow. I didn't know how yet, but Brighid could help me find a spell or - or *something*! Pip paced restlessly as I dressed. I grabbed the cord of the amulet, and without considering what I was doing, I draped it around my neck. There was an odd tickling sensation where the stone touched my skin and I reached my hand to my chest, but the amulet wasn't there. I glanced up at my mirror, and pulled the neck of my blouse down. Where the amulet had touched my skin, it had disappeared leaving only the raised outline of the triskele design, as it had done when Alex wore it.

I clutched at that spot on my skin in a panic, thinking somehow that I'd lost the only connection to Alex, but then I felt the sentience, soothing me, despite it's own franticness. *How am I going to find him?!* I thought, stifling the urge to scream. *I don't know where to start! I don't even know how this thing works!*

The room seemed to tilt slightly then, throwing me off balance and I wobbled, trying to keep from toppling over. And then, everything was still again. Only, I wasn't in my bedroom. I was in what looked like a study. Book shelves lined the entirety of one wall. I was standing in the center of this new room. At one end was a bank of windows overlooking an apple orchard in the twilight, a closed door at the opposite end. I turned away from the bank of bookshelves to the other side of the room. In the corner near the windows was a desk. There was someone sitting at the desk, facing away from me toward the windows. It was a woman with dark hair twisted up into a bun held fast by a couple of pencils. I gasped slightly at the shock of seeing someone else in this strange room. The lady stiffened, startled as well. She turned to look at me. She was a small woman, with skin the color of milky tea, a pair of dark-rimmed glasses perched on her nose with a beaded chain attached to the temples so that they could be easily worn around the neck. Her eyes went wide and she stood to face me.

"Morgaine?" she said. "How did you…" She looked at me closely and quickly closed the distance between us. "What's wrong, child?" I knew her then. Dressed not in a blue shift, but in jeans and a lilac blouse. Her eyes were the same gorgeous shade of green, and the woad crescent was between her brows.

"Lady?" It was definitely Morgaine of the Fae. I heard the door open behind us.

"Morgaine, I just had —" a man had entered and now stood looking from me to Morgaine. "Who is this?" The newcomer was tall with sandy, slightly unkempt, not quite shoulder-length hair. He wore dark slacks and a black shirt with a cleric's collar. He studied me with suspicion.

"Brother Rhys, this is my namesake, Morgaine Clemenson. She is the witch who recently aided our Alex with a banishment. Brother Rhys is a founder of Tempus Scolarium– it's what we call our society," she added, in answer to my questioning look.

Brother Rhys narrowed his eyes. "She shouldn't be here." He turned his attention to me. "How did you get here?"

I felt a tickling at my chest and reached down to find that the amulet had materialized. I pulled it from my neck and held it out to Morgaine. "I was awakened by…this. There's something wrong - Alex is in danger. I can't understand it all, it's too overwhelming, the images and sensations. But, it brought me here."

Morgaine didn't take the amulet from me, but laid her hand over it and closed her eyes.

"This is highly unorthodox," Brother Rhys began, but Morgaine held her other hand up to silence him.

After a few moments she opened her eyes. "Alex has been taken. He is no longer on this plane."

"Oh, oh, no. Please. Where is he?"

"I fear he is among the demons, love." She put a hand on my shoulder.

"No. There must be something we can do. I won't accept that he's just gone."

Brother Rhys shook his head. "There is nothing to be done. If he can't get himself out of this mess—"

"Rhys!" Morgaine said sharply. She turned her attention to me again. "We will do all we can to help him, I promise."

I looked at Brother Rhys and narrowed my eyes.

He sighed. "Yes. We will try. I give you my word as well. But if he is on the demons' plane, there may not be a way. In any event, you can't stay."

"But," I looked pleadingly at Morgaine, "I want to help. I can't just not do anything."

"Go home, and hope for the best," Brother Rhys said. "Even if we do get him back, you'd never see him again anyway."

I looked at Morgaine again. I didn't need to say anything, the softness in her eyes told me that she knew. Alex and I were in love, regardless of the Tempus Scolarium rules and restrictions.

I don't think Brother Rhys noticed. "Really my dear, I know this is all very new and interesting, but it's time for you to return to where you belong." He spoke to me as if speaking to a child who'd just wandered into a chocolate factory.

"I believe I can help find Alex. Please, won't you let me try?" I kept my voice even. I did not want to seem to be begging.

"The situation is well in hand Miss Clemenson," he said. "We'll see you safely back to your own time and place. I'll take that."

As he stepped forward and reached for the Tempus Purus, the stone began to tremble in my hand, and the three of us flinched as a loud, piercing shriek sounded within our heads, accompanied by a stabbing pain behind the eyes. It stopped only when the man dropped his hand and stepped back.

"No, I don't believe you will take it, Brother Rhys." Morgaine peered at the Tempus Purus, now stilled, in my hand. "We shall have to come at this problem another way." Her eyes met mine. "Welcome to Avalon, Morgaine."

If you enjoyed this book and would like to be informed of future releases, please visit www.moonmaidenbooks.com.

Keep reading for a preview of "Seeking Truths", book 2 of the Time Traveling Demon Hunter series!

Acknowledgments

Many thanks to my critique partner, Brigid, for her insightful thoughts on the text through the varying drafts. And to my editor, Graham, who ruthlessly "blue-penciled" the debris of my comma addiction, helped me polish my grammar, and made sure my Victorian gentleman didn't sound too much like a modern hipster. A special shout-out to Margie and Eric at Relax Inn in Nags Head, NC, whose lovely accommodations encouraged the good night's sleep in which the kernel of this story was dreamt into being. Also, super-duper special thanks to Julie Clemenson - without whom none of this would have been possible, *obviously*.

And, thank *you*, for reading my book! I hope you've enjoyed it. If so, I would be grateful if you would leave a review on the site you purchased the book from, and/or on Goodreads. Please tell your friends if you know they would enjoy the story - indie authors depend on word of mouth to help generate interest in their work. If you would like to keep in touch, you can follow my page on Facebook: http://www.facebook.com/MELaytonBooks, sign up for the mailing list at http://www.moonmaidenbooks.com, and you can reach me by email at ItsMaryHerself@gmail.com.

Seeking Truths (Preview)

"Avalon", Morgaine had called this place. The venerable Lady of Avalon, with the exception of her regal bearing and the woad crescent tattooed between her brows, looked nothing like the legend and everything like a modern business woman. After my sudden appearance in her study, she had taken me on a tour of the grounds. Her colleague, Brother Rhys, still fuming about my unexpected arrival and refusal to quietly go away, had left to call a meeting of the board of the Tempus Scolarium.

As we stood outside the dormitory - actually a large converted manor house - I fingered the leather cord around my neck holding the Tempus Purus amulet whose magic had brought me here. I could still feel a trace of its sentient presence in the back of my mind, but it seemed to be only waiting and watching now. Until a few hours ago, it had belonged to the time-traveling demon hunter, Alexander Ramsey, who'd left me - presumably forever - after we'd vanquished an incubus back to the demonic plane from the small town I live in on the coast of North Carolina's Outer Banks. Against all the rules and restrictions of his time-traveling order, we had fallen in love. His Tempus Purus had materialized to me weeks after he'd gone, bombarded my consciousness with a jumble of images and impressions of Alex in danger, and now I was standing next to a fragrant apple grove on what I was assured was truly the storied isle of Avalon.

I stared at the design carved on the front of the building above the door. Like the symbol on the amulet I wore, it was a triskele with a triquetra within its center. Unlike the amulet, the arms of the triskele ended in simple spirals. I peered down at the carved stone around my neck. Its arms ended in graceful acanthus leaf curves.

Morgaine noticed my confusion. "The design is slightly different for all of us." She held up her own Tempus Purus. The arms of her triskele curved into a design reminiscent of the branches of the apple trees surrounding us, with fruits at the ends of the boughs. "When we first discovered the amulets, all of them had a design like the one you see there." She pointed to the building. "But, we found that once they bound themselves to each of us, the design changed. Something that always seems to suit the person it is attuned to."

I turned away from the door and looked around the immediate grounds. There were a few smaller buildings nearby, and paths leading off into the lush greenery surrounding the area and into dense, hilly forests. A tor rose above the trees, probably a half a mile or so away, near the center of the isle. Beyond that, nothing was visible. A thick mist surrounded the entire island. Despite that, it was bright, as if the mists parted above us just for the sun and moon to shine their light upon the isle.

"Is the mist always there?" I asked.

"Yes. Never above, but always around."

"What if I were to walk in a straight line toward the mist? Where would I go?"

The Lady of Avalon chuckled. "You'd end up right back here. Eventually. The mists protect us, and there is no way off the isle by walking into them. No matter how many times you try, you would always end up where you started. The mists would always bring you home."

"This isn't my home," I said, and instantly regretted my tone. Whatever was happening wasn't the fault of Morgaine, or this isle. I turned to her, about to apologize, but she silenced me with a gesture.

"No, it isn't. But, you are its guest for now, and it will protect you as one of its own." She gave me an understanding smile. "When did you know you loved him?"

I thought back on the events of the previous couple of months. A crisis meant the two of us had to perform a ritual to replace a destroyed fetish, a carving of a magical creature, that was instrumental to the success of the banishment of the demon. It required sex magic, and despite our having only met weeks before, it was astonishingly natural, and highly successful. The fetish Alex had recreated during the ritual seemed to bond with both of us and had not only performed its intended duty, but lent extra potency to my magic when I feared I would be too weak to trap the demon we needed to banish. The experience had been extraordinary. I nearly stumbled over some of the words, so impassioned was I during the ritual. It was obvious to me then that Alex had captured my heart, but on further reflection, there was always something between us. "When he first walked through the door," I said. "Our eyes locked and there was an instant connection. I think I denied it for a long time, though." I bit back the emotion that rose within me. "Maybe too long."

Morgaine reached out and pushed my hair back from my face, her hand lingering as she brushed a tear away before it could finish its journey down my cheek. "I'm sorry, dearest," she said. "I suspect you probably already know it, at least in your heart, but he loves you, too."

I was grateful that she used the present tense. Brother Rhys was all too ready to strike Alex off as already dead, but I refused to believe it. "He never said, but I felt it. In his touch, in the way he looked at me." And, when the amulet came to me, its sentience connected with me somehow and allowed me to know Alex's final thoughts before he had to leave me. "*I will never stop trying to come back. I love you.*"

She nodded. "I suspected, when he returned, that you had stolen his heart." She placed a hand on my shoulder. "I promise you, whatever the board decides, I will do everything in my power to help you bring him back."

The door opened. "Morgaine," Brother Rhys called.

"Yes?" Morgaine and I said in unison, both turning to him.

He rolled his eyes, and huffed in frustration. "Something must be done to tell the two of you apart. You can't both be Morgaine."

"You can call me Mora," I said. "It's my friend's nickname for me."

Brother Rhys gave a single brisk nod. "Morgaine," he said again, pointedly addressing my hostess, "the board will meet two hours hence."

***

Two hours later, Morgaine led me into a reception room within the same building as her study. A banquet table in the middle of the room was laden with fruits, cheeses, sweetmeats, and baked goods, and glass pitchers of water and another liquid with a rich honey color which I guessed to be a fruit juice of some sort. There were ten others milling about, talking in hushed tones. The walls were paneled, lending a warmth to the room, and as I looked around, I noticed they were covered in portraits. Morgaine was there, as were the others in the room. Brother Rhys stared disdainfully down from his portrait beside Morgaine's. The man himself stood across the room, his back to us, in conversation with a man whose portrait was on the other side of Morgaine's. Other paintings were of men and women who were not in the room with us, and as my gaze fell to my right, a familiar face gazed back at me. The portrait of Alex was so life-like, I felt I could have reached out and taken his hand. His dark, shoulder-length hair was loose, the way I'd come to prefer it, and the artist had done an amazing job of capturing his beautiful, flashing blue eyes. Despite the casualness of his hairstyle, he wore his Victorian Royal Navy dress uniform with a bearing that made him look like a prince, and there was even a ceremonial sword at his waist.

"Many of those you see are occupied with duties elsewhere on the isle. Others, like Alex, are away on missions involving the breach of the demonic gate wards. Those present," she nodded toward the others in the room, "are members of the board."

My eyes traveled back around the room again, taking in those around us. There were seven women, not including myself, and four men. The man in conversation with Brother Rhys was looking our way. He caught my eye and gave me a kind smile. He was dressed similarly to Brother Rhys in dark slacks and black shirt, but lacked the cleric's collar.

Morgaine leaned in and whispered, "That is Tal. He acts as president of the board, although we don't really have a strict hierarchy."

"Tal…Taliesin?" Was I about to meet another legend, I wondered.

She smiled. "I see you've read your Arthurian legends. Yes, that is the Welsh bard Taliesin, although we just call him Tal." I thought back to some accounts I'd read that had Morgaine and Taliesin as lovers. Morgaine must have read my mind. "And, yes, we have been lovers." She squared her shoulders as Brother Rhys noticed us. "I'll tell you all about it later." She winked and then linked her arm in mine as Brother Rhys stalked toward us.

"She can't be here," he said, shortly.

"This meeting concerns her, Rhys. She has every right to be here." Morgaine's tone suggested she would brook no argument. Luckily, she didn't have to. Tal had followed Brother Rhys.

"I agree, Rhys," he said, bright hazel eyes beneath a fringe of milk chocolate brown hair lighting on me briefly before he turned his attention back to Brother Rhys. "We can't expect to decide the lady's fate without her input. Or that of the amulet's - I understand it does not wish to be parted from her." The corner of his mouth quirked up in amusement and at the same time, I felt a tingle as if the amulet at my breast were voicing its agreement. It seems word of the incident had got around. When Brother Rhys had tried to take the amulet earlier, it reacted by inflicting a loud noise and a sharp pain behind the eyes to all in the room, ending only when Brother Rhys had stepped away.

Brother Rhys said nothing, merely darting an irritated glance at me and heaving a snappish sigh before turning to walk away. I felt certain that if he would have opened his mouth to speak, he would have uttered a peevish "What - ever". That thought nearly made me giggle, and served to slightly ease the bundle of tension knotted in my belly. As we made our way across the room toward the open double doors leading into the meeting room, Tal paused and poured a glass of the amber liquid. "I do hope you'll try this, Mora," he said, offering me the glass. "It will fortify you and," he leaned in conspiratorially, "calm your nerves."

"Thank you," I said, taking the glass and returning his smile. I glanced at Morgaine as we proceeded into the meeting room. With a small smile and a bow of her head, she assured me that I had at least two friends amongst the board members.

About the Author

M. E. Layton is a North Carolina native. She has been an actress, a DJ, and some other less interesting things during her lifetime. In addition to writing fiction, she is also an accomplished artist with artwork in collections throughout the world. She is married to an Englishman and they enjoy travelling within the US and to Europe.

You can connect with her online at:
melayton.weebly.com
www.facebook.com/MELaytonBooks
www.facebook.com/MaryLaytonArt
www.twitter.com/Rhiamon